CITY FARM

Darren and Basher

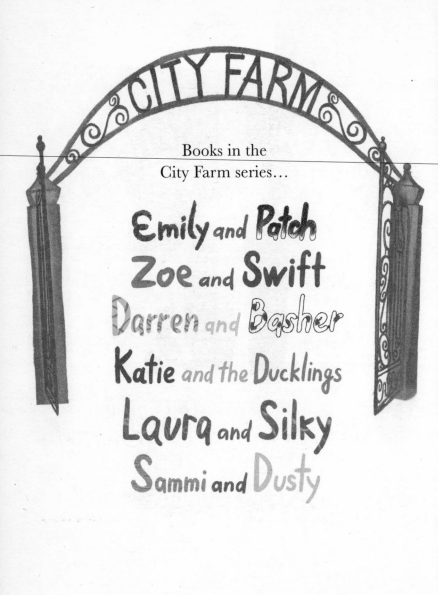

Books in the
City Farm series...

Darren and Basher

Jessie Williams

Special thanks to
Thea Bennett

First published in 2013 by Curious Fox,
an imprint of Capstone Global Library Limited,
7 Pilgrim Street, London, EC4V 6LB
Registered company number: 6695582

www.curious-fox.com

Text © Hothouse Fiction Ltd 2013

Series created by Hothouse Fiction
www.hothousefiction.com

The author's moral rights are hereby asserted.

Illustrations by Dewi@kja-artists

All characters in this publication are fictitious and any resemblance
to real persons, living or dead, is purely coincidental.

ISBN 978 1 78202 022 6

1 3 5 7 9 10 8 6 4 2

A CIP catalogue for this book is available from the British Library.

Typeset in Baskerville by Hothouse Fiction Ltd

Printed and bound in the United Kingdom by CPI

For Owen and Billy.

Prologue

Art was Darren's favourite lesson. At least it was, until the day a man with a black beard came into the art room, carrying a large bowl of fruit. Darren had never seen him before.

'Where's Miss Hastings?' Darren asked.

Miss Hastings was the teacher who usually took the art class. She really liked Darren's artwork, and always had something good to say about it.

'You've got a great imagination, Darren,' she frequently told him, and sometimes she added: 'The way you use colours is fantastic.'

Art was the only thing he was any good at, since he'd first started at the secondary school, two years ago.

The black-bearded man plonked the bowl down in front of the class. It contained a bunch of grapes and a large melon.

'Making a fruit salad, sir?' asked Darren's mate Gary, who was sitting next to him.

The man frowned at Gary. 'Less of the cheek,' he said. Then he looked at Darren. 'Miss Hastings is off sick. Nothing serious, but she'll be away for the last two weeks of term. I'm Mr Dodge. I'll be taking over from today.'

'OK,' Darren said. Something told him he wasn't going to enjoy this new teacher's lessons. They wouldn't be fun, like Miss Hastings' lessons were.

He got out his rainbow-coloured felt-tips and laid them on the table in front of him. He always brought his own pens to the art class. With them, he could create the graffiti-style, super-bright effects he liked. He'd rather have used his spray cans, but they weren't allowed at school.

'You won't be needing those,' Mr Dodge said, eyeing the pens.

'But I always—' Darren began.

'Today you're going to be drawing a still life in pencil. The result must be realistic. It must reflect exactly what you see.'

Darren hated using pencils to draw. They were so dull and grey. And they were always breaking too.

'Still-life drawing is the foundation of all great art,' Mr Dodge said, as he walked around the class giving out paper and pencils. 'Da Vinci, Raphael, Picasso – they all began with the simple still life. I'll demonstrate for you.'

He set up an easel with a sheet of paper on it at the front of the class. Then he peered at the fruit bowl, and began sketching.

Darren sighed. This was so boring. He looked at Gary and yawned.

Gary sniggered. 'Let's go and smash that melon in,' he hissed. 'That'll make it more exciting.'

'Quiet!' Mr Dodge called. 'Still-life drawing requires concentration.'

Darren picked up the pencil he'd been given. He tried to copy exactly the way the melon looked, sitting on top of the fruit bowl, but he didn't like the way it came out. It looked lifeless, like something out of an art textbook.

He pushed harder with the pencil, trying to make a darker line, and the point snapped off.

'Sir, my pencil broke,' he said.

'Sharpen it, then,' Mr Dodge answered, still sketching.

Darren didn't have a pencil sharpener. He looked

around the class, but everyone was busy drawing. He didn't want to interrupt Mr Dodge again, so he got one of his felt-tips out. A bright purple one.

He used it to sketch the bunch of grapes. The cluster of shapes reminded him of a group of kids all huddled together in the playground, so he drew faces on them.

'Nice one, Daz!' Gary whispered, peering over his shoulder.

Darren turned his attention to the melon. He drew a big circle with a yellow felt-tip. Then he had an idea. He got a black pen, and added a beard and a pair of bushy eyebrows to the melon shape he'd just drawn.

It looked very like Mr Dodge now. Darren gave him arms, and a long paintbrush in one hand, as if the teacher had just painted the grape-kids' cheeky little faces.

Gary peered over Darren's shoulder and snorted with laughter.

Mr Dodge left the front of the class and came down to Darren's table. All the kids in the art class were looking at him, their eyes wide.

'Very amusing,' Mr Dodge said in his deep voice. 'But not what I asked you to do, is it?'

'It's loads better than your dumb drawing, sir. Daz

is a genius,' Gary piped up.

'Right, you, get out!' the teacher shouted. 'I won't have disrespect in my classroom. Go to the headmaster's office!'

Gary got up and shuffled out of the art room, turning to wink at Darren as he opened the door.

'Now, young man,' Mr Dodge continued, staring at Darren from under his bushy eyebrows. 'Either you do as you're told, or you'll be sent out too. An art class is no place for this kind of stupid scribbling.'

Darren felt anger bubble up inside of him. This was the one lesson he did well in. Now it was going to be just like all the rest. 'What do you know about art anyway?' he shouted, jumping up from his chair.

'Quite a lot, actually,' the teacher began. 'My paintings are very well known ...'

But Darren wasn't listening. He didn't wait to be sent to the headmaster for being cheeky. He just ran out of the classroom, and hid behind the bike shed until it was time to go home.

Darren went to bed early, but he couldn't sleep. It was one of those nights in the middle of summer when it doesn't get properly dark until very late. He lay in bed, turning from side to side.

Mr Dodge's booming voice echoed in his ears. '*Stupid scribbling!*' Darren heard him say, over and over again.

But his graffiti-style felt-tip drawing was just as lifelike, just as realistic in its own way as the teacher's pencil sketch! It was so frustrating to be told off like that, for doing something that he knew he was good at.

At eleven o'clock, Darren heard his dad coming to bed. His mum was at work. She'd left just after tea to go to her night shift at the hospital. Soon his dad's snores could be heard through the bedroom wall. They were so loud they seemed to be shaking the whole flat.

Darren slid out of bed and put on his trackie bottoms and his trainers. Then he pulled his favourite hoodie over his head and picked up the shoulder bag with his spray cans in. There was only one way he was going to get Mr Dodge's voice out of his head.

He tiptoed out of his bedroom and went to the kitchen. The window in there looked out onto the walkway that ran outside all the flats on his floor. It was easy to open it and climb out.

He made his way through the silent, dark streets until he came to the entrance to his school. A light was on in one of the school's windows. Someone must have forgotten to switch it off, even though there were notices in every classroom reminding you to turn the light out when you left.

Darren made his way to the bike shed. Behind it was a long concrete wall. He'd seen it earlier, when he was hiding there. Darren's heart beat fast, like it always did when he was about to create a piece of art. He got out a green spray can and shook it.

Then he reached up as high as he could and began to outline some jagged shapes on the wall – palm tree leaves. In what seemed like only a few moments the concrete was transformed into a lush, green jungle.

Next, Darren grabbed a red spray can and began sketching in a troop of monkeys, swinging through the trees. He added a bigger monkey – himself, with his hoodie pulled forward to hide his face – chasing them with a spray can.

At the top he added *ART RULES* in big, bubble-style writing, and at the bottom he put his own special tag: *DAZ*. He always wrote this tag in hard-to-read, spiky letters, so that only someone who really understood graffiti would be able to read them.

He was just finishing the *Z* when he heard footsteps approaching. Someone must have spotted him!

Darren ran for the school gates, stuffing the spray cans back into the bag as he went. He was too late.

'Darren Taylor? Stop! What're you doing here at this time of night?'

It was the headmaster. He must've been working late. He always had to put in extra hours when he was working out the timetable for the next school year.

'You know that vandalizing school property is a very serious offence?' the headmaster said, coming up to Darren.

Darren shivered. If only he'd left the bike shed as soon as he'd finished drawing, and not added his tag. What was going to happen to him now?

 14

Chapter One

'How's it going, Asha?'

Kerry, the project co-ordinator on the City Farm Harvest Hope project, came into the barn with a paper cup full of orange juice. 'You've been sketching away for ages.'

'I'm not sure.' Asha looked at the drawing she'd just done. It was of Dusty, the grumpy old grey donkey who'd been at the farm for many years.

The drawing still wasn't right. She'd spent all morning on it, but it didn't look much like Dusty. She wished she'd never offered to help out with designing the posters for City Farm's Rare Breeds Show, which was happening in a week's time.

'You're doing a great job,' Kerry said, handing over the juice. 'It's great that the posters are being done by

 15

one of the young people involved in the project.'

'Thanks!' Asha said, and took a sip of juice. It was really cool and refreshing. After she finished drinking she got up from the sofa and stretched her legs. She was feeling very stiff after sitting down for so long.

'Oh, look!' Kerry said, picking up the drawing. 'It's Curly, isn't it? I love the way you've made her look so woolly.'

Asha bit her lip. Curly was the farm's Dartmoor sheep, and she didn't look a bit like Dusty. She was much fatter and had a thick coat of white wool.

Asha stared at her drawing again. Maybe she should add a bit of brown to Dusty's fur. And make his legs a bit longer.

'Well – must dash!' Kerry tossed her long, beaded plaits over her shoulder. 'We're inundated with visitors today. The sunshine always brings them out to see the animals. Don't sit in here for too long, Asha. It's gorgeous outside.'

Asha nodded, reaching for the brown crayon. She shaded over Dusty's body to make it darker. She also tried to make his fur look smooth, so it was less like Curly's thick wool. He still didn't look right.

'Why're you hiding in here?' Asha's friend Jack called, peering in through the door. 'I've just been showing off Cynthia's dribbling skills to some kids. She was a star.'

Cynthia, the Tamworth pig, was Jack's favourite animal at the farm. Thanks to his clever training, she had some really cool football skills.

Asha sighed. Bright sunlight streamed in through the barn's high windows. She'd much rather be outside playing football with Jack and Cynthia.

'I've got to finish this,' she said. 'The Rare Breeds Show posters have got to be ready in a week's time, and I've only done one so far.'

'Hey, let me see!' Jack picked up her drawing. 'Oh, Asha!' he said, his face turning pink with delight. 'It's brilliant!'

'Really?' Asha stared at him.

'She's not quite the right colour, but—'

'Right colour…?' Asha stammered. Her drawing just *couldn't* look like Curly any more. Not after all the changes she'd made.

'…you could always go over her with an orange crayon,' Jack continued. 'I'm really chuffed you chose Cynthia for the first poster.'

Asha sighed. Cynthia was ginger in colour. And a pig. She looked nothing like Dusty at all.

'What's wrong, Asha?' Jack asked.

'Nothing.' Asha turned the drawing over so he couldn't see it any more. 'It's not ready yet. I need to add the finishing touches.'

Jack nodded. 'I'd better get back to the pigsty. I promised Cynthia an extra-large apple, for being such a star. See you later!'

Asha watched, as he hurried off to the café to get the apple. Part of her wanted to run and join him, but she couldn't, she had a job to do, even if no one could tell what she was drawing. Maybe she'd made Dusty look *too* smooth. After all, his fur was quite long, even in summer. She scribbled over his body with the brown crayon, trying to create a fluffy, furry effect.

'Hello, lass!'

Asha looked up and saw Rory, the farm manager, coming into the barn. His white hair was sticking up all over the place, as usual, and his face was redder than ever from being out in the sunshine all day long, looking after the visitors to the farm.

He headed straight for the water cooler in the corner of the barn and helped himself to a drink.

'Can I show you my poster design?' Asha asked him.

'You can,' Rory said, in between gulps of water from a paper cup. 'But I'm not much of an artist.'

Asha held up her drawing.

'Very nice indeed,' Rory said. 'What is it, lass?'

Asha sighed. 'What does it look like?' she asked.

'Well.' Rory peered at the paper with his head on one side. 'It's got four legs, two ears and a lot of brown fur. So I guess it's one of the animals.'

'Which one?'

'Um? Now you've got me.' Rory stroked his chin thoughtfully. 'I would say – since you're so fond of them – that it's probably one of the guinea pigs.'

Asha was so disappointed she couldn't speak.

'Ah. Wrong answer, of course!' Rory said in a kind voice. 'But you shouldn't take any notice of me. I told you I wasn't much of an artist. It's got great fur though.'

'It's Dusty!' Asha told him.

'Ah, right.' Rory nodded. 'Yes. I see it now. Those are *hooves*, aren't they? Not paws. How stupid of me.'

Asha almost felt like crying, and it wasn't like her to cry. All the long months she'd been ill and miserable with leukaemia, she'd hardly cried at all. It was just so frustrating not being able to draw a really good poster design to advertise the show. If lots of people came, there would be more money for City Farm, and Asha knew how important that was.

'You know what,' Rory said after a moment. 'You

might find it easier if you actually had Dusty in front of you when you were drawing him. That'd be better than trying to remember what he looks like.'

Asha suddenly felt a whole lot better. 'Great! I'll take him to the vegetable garden, out of the way of all the visitors, and tie him to one of the apple trees!'

'Exactly.' Rory nodded. 'I bet the old fellow will be happy as a pig in muck, standing in the shade while you sketch him.'

Dusty was in the field shelter with City Farm's horse and pony, Swift and Stanley. They liked to stand in there and doze on a hot day, out of the sun. He wasn't very keen to leave his friends and go with Asha, and he walked very slowly as she led him along the path.

'It's all right, Dusty. Once we get to the garden you can relax,' she told him.

Dusty stopped and looked over his shoulder, back towards his friends. 'Ee-yore!' he brayed. And then he did it again, even louder.

A family was walking down the path towards Asha.

'Why's that donkey making so much noise?' one of the kids, a little boy, asked.

'Poor old thing.' His mum smiled at Asha. 'Perhaps he's got a tummy-ache.'

'He's fine,' Asha said, feeling very embarrassed. 'He's always noisy. He's just being stubborn. Come on, Dusty!' She tugged on his lead rope and Dusty let out another loud bray.

Now a group of older boys were laughing at her. 'Wanna push to get him started?' one of them shouted.

Asha tugged on the rope, but Dusty just rolled his eyes at her and dug his hooves into the path.

'You're really showing me up, Dusty!' Asha whispered.

There was half a flapjack in her pocket, left over from her morning snack. She got it out, and waved it in front of the donkey's nose.

He pricked his long, furry ears and started walking again. The boys cheered and whooped. Asha breathed a big sigh of relief.

When they got to the vegetable garden, Asha tied Dusty's lead rope to the trunk of the apple tree and sat down on a bench. Now at last she could get on with her drawing.

But after being so slow all the way there, Dusty suddenly livened up. 'Ee-yore!' he brayed, pulling on the rope.

'You're supposed to be standing still!' Asha called to him.

Dusty ignored her and carried on pulling. The tree shook, and a couple of apples fell to the ground.

Dusty stopped pulling to sniff at them. Then he started crunching on one of the fruit with his long yellow teeth. Asha grabbed her pencil and began sketching. The only problem was that Dusty's head was down. He wouldn't look very good on a poster with his nose on the ground, scoffing apples.

Asha called the donkey's name and snapped her fingers. He lifted his head to look at her, then he started walking round the tree to hunt for more apples.

This is great! Asha thought, scribbling away. She outlined Dusty's long ears, and the shape of his furry body. Rory had been right. Even with Dusty moving around, he was much easier to draw now that she could see him.

Once the outline was done, Asha got her brown crayon to colour it in. She concentrated on this for a few moments, until Dusty interrupted her.

'Eeee-yore!' he roared.

He had circled the tree so many times that the rope had got wound round it until there was none left. He was caught with his head right up against the trunk.

He rolled his eyes at Asha, as if to say 'Help!'

'Oh, Dusty!' She burst out laughing. 'You're hilarious.'

Now at last he was standing still, but Asha couldn't concentrate on drawing any more. She put down her pad and laughed and laughed. Then she saw how unhappy Dusty looked, so she rushed over to untangle him. She tried to lead him back round the tree again so the rope would unwind, but he wouldn't move. Finally she unclipped the lead rope from his halter so she could untwist the rope herself.

As soon as she did this, Dusty spotted another apple and dropped his nose down to eat it. Asha was taken by surprise and let go of the halter.

When he realized he was free, Dusty seemed to forget he was a grumpy old donkey. To Asha's horror, he kicked his heels in the air and bolted across the garden, trampling over the rows of lettuces that were growing there. He pushed the gate open with his nose and galloped up the path to his field, leaving Asha holding the rope.

She ran to the path, just in time to see the family who'd spoken to her earlier scattering out of the way as Dusty charged past them. There was no way Asha was going to be able to stop the bolting donkey.

'Oh, no!' Asha cried.

'What's going on?' Kerry called, hurrying up the path.

Asha explained that Dusty had escaped. 'I was drawing him from life, but he just wouldn't stay still!'

Kerry smiled. 'Poor old Dusty. He must've been feeling lonely without his mates. I'll go and let him back into the field. Never mind, Asha. It's almost time to finish up for the afternoon anyway. You'll have better luck with your drawing tomorrow.'

'OK,' Asha said, but she didn't feel very hopeful.

Dusty would probably be his usual grumpy old self again and refuse to do what she wanted. And how likely was it that she would suddenly become a genius at art?

'In your dreams, Asha Gupta!' she said to herself, and went back to the barn to collect her things so that Kerry could give her a lift home.

Chapter Two

'You'd better behave while you're here,' Darren's dad said, as he, Darren and Darren's mum arrived outside the gates of City Farm.

Darren wished they'd come in the car. It wasn't far from the block of flats where he lived with his parents, but if they'd driven he could've ducked down in the back seat, and no one would've seen him.

It was embarrassing enough that he'd been suspended from school for the last two weeks of term, then told he must spend the first two weeks of his summer holiday on the farm, at the Harvest Hope project – or risk being permanently excluded from school.

Darren looked back over his shoulder, towards the flats. Luckily, there was no one about. If his friends

Gary and Steven, who lived on the estate, saw him hanging around here, they'd really make fun of him.

He'd never been to City Farm before, but he knew it was a place for kids who were soppy about animals. Not teenagers, like he'd become a few weeks ago on his thirteenth birthday.

There were some pictures of the farm animals on the sign that hung above the gate. They were really naff. Just the sort of cutesy stuff that grown-ups thought kids liked.

'I shouldn't be here, Dad,' he said. 'It's meant for little kids.'

His dad's face turned red. 'Perhaps you'll think twice then, next time you decide to behave like one!' he snapped.

Darren's dad used to be a sergeant in the army. When he was angry, he still sounded like one. It was best to go along with him when he was in that mood, however much you might want to argue.

'Lots of kids get expelled for doing what you did – vandalizing your own school,' his dad continued. 'So you'd better use your time here as a chance to give up all that art nonsense.'

Darren bit his lip. His dad didn't approve of art. He thought it was all right for a hobby, but a complete waste of time as a lesson. And he *hated* graffiti. He wanted Darren to concentrate on what he called 'useful' subjects, like maths.

Inside the farmyard, Darren could see some chickens running about, and a horse looking over a stable door. He sniffed. There was a strong smell of manure.

'It's a bit whiffy,' he said.

His mum put her arm through his. 'Farmyard perfume, Daz,' she said. 'It's a lovely smell.'

Darren's mum had grown up on a farm in Ireland. She hadn't been back there since before Darren was born, but she liked to remember the happy times she had there, when she was a little girl.

'Shut up, Mum!' Darren whispered.

She quite often embarrassed him with the weird things she came out with. He wished she hadn't woken up early from her after-work sleep and decided to come along.

But there was no stopping her today.

'Look at that,' she sighed, pointing to a ramshackle barn that stood next to the farmyard. 'It must have been there for hundreds of years. Doesn't it look just like an old mother hen, crouching there and watching over all the people coming and going?'

'No, it looks like a half-falling-down old building,' Darren replied. His mum really was bonkers sometimes.

He walked away, so he wouldn't have to listen to any more of her craziness. He stared up at the barn. It was the oddest building he'd ever seen. There wasn't a straight line, or a square corner anywhere. Not like the flats where he lived, which were all perfect rectangles, with no curves at all. It was more like a living thing than a building in its shape, he thought. Maybe his mum wasn't so mad after all. The crooked roof of the barn did look a bit like a bird's wings, held out to protect its chicks.

He quite liked this idea now. He'd brought some pens with him, hidden in the bottom of his bag. *Maybe he'd get a chance to do some drawing later…*

This thought was interrupted as the barn's beak – or rather its front door – opened. A boy with sandy hair came out, carrying a bucket. He looked shyly at Darren and his mum and dad.

'The office is in there,' he said, pointing inside the barn. And then he hurried off with the bucket.

Darren felt a rush of panic. Was he really going to be stuck here for the next two weeks, shovelling manure and nattering about animals with kids like that?

'Dad, don't make me stay,' he stammered. 'I'll work really hard at my lessons, I promise. Whatever you want.'

'Bit late for that,' Dad said, and led the way into the barn.

'Hello, there!' An old guy with a red face got up from a desk to greet them. His white hair was all over the place, floppy and wild. It reminded Darren of the mop his mum washed the kitchen floor with.

'This is Darren,' his dad said. 'Darren Taylor.'

The mop-man grinned at Darren. 'Great stuff,' he said. 'We could do with a big tall lad like yourself to help out. We've got a busy time ahead. I'm Rory, by the way. The farm manager.'

Darren's mum nudged his arm to remind him of his manners.

'Hi,' he muttered.

'You must be Darren!' A young black woman with a big smile came to join the white-haired man. 'I'm Kerry, the co-ordinator for the Harvest Hope project.'

Darren cringed as she said this. He remembered what the policeman who'd come to the school had said: 'You need the Harvest Hope treatment, son. Works miracles with antisocial lads like you. Let's hope they can take you on.'

The only miracle that Darren wished for now was one that would make the floor of the barn open up and swallow him alive. But it didn't happen, of course.

Rory sat down again and picked up a pile of papers. 'Kerry will sort you out, Darren,' he said. 'I've got a mountain of admin to get through for our Rare Breeds Show. We've got a load of new animals coming to visit.'

Kerry led them over to her desk. She was almost cool, Darren thought, in a pop star kind of way, with her plaits and her ripped jeans and her leopard-spotted boots. But no one who worked on a farm could ever be properly cool.

'I'll be glad when all this is sorted out,' his dad said. 'I suppose you'll want us to sign something.'

'That's right,' Kerry said. 'It won't take long.' She picked up a file with Darren's name on the front.

Darren wanted to snatch it out of her hands and rip it up. He hated the idea of her reading all about his 'antisocial behaviour' – when all he'd been doing was his art.

Kerry glanced up at him, as if she'd read his thoughts. 'Don't worry,' she said. 'It's just a formality. You'll soon feel at home.'

Never, Darren thought to himself.

He went over and sat on one of the big sofas on the other side of the barn. He didn't need to stand there and watch while his parents signed away the next two weeks of his life.

Suddenly, there was a loud honk from a car horn. *Paarp! Parp-paaarp!* Someone must have driven into the farmyard.

'Aha!' Rory jumped to his feet. 'Another delivery!'

He hurried out of the barn, leaving the papers in a jumble all over his desk.

Kerry was still talking to his mum and dad. Darren leaned back on the sofa. But there was no chance for him to relax. Something was really kicking off outside. A dog started barking, and Darren could hear people shouting.

'Help! I can't hold him!' a woman squealed.

'I told you not to get him out yet!' a man yelled, sounding really annoyed.

'Ouch!' That sounded like Rory, the farm manager, shouting in pain.

Darren grinned. It sounded like mayhem. He had to go and have a look.

As he opened the door, a black and white tornado shot past. Darren blinked in surprise. On closer inspection, the tornado turned out to be a small goat with two little horns on top of his head and a pointed white beard under his chin.

Darren couldn't help laughing as the little creature charged round and round like an out-of-control skateboarder, his hooves skidding across the yard.

In the middle of the yard was a car with a trailer attached. A woman was leaning on the bonnet, clutching her wrist. Next to her, Rory was standing on one leg, rubbing his shin. Beside him, two men in overalls spun round like clockwork toys as they turned to watch the goat race around the farmyard.

'Hey, mate!' Darren called, as the animal shot past him again.

Boing! The goat leaped in the air, bouncing like a black and white rubber ball.

One of the men made a grab for him, and the goat leaped again. This time he landed with a crash on the bonnet of the car.

'Help!' squeaked the woman.

'Meh-eh-eh!' said the goat, standing proudly on the car bonnet and gazing all around the farmyard with shining eyes.

'Calm down, lad,' Rory said, limping towards the goat and holding out his hand. 'Take it easy.'

The goat looked at him with disdain. He sprang off the car and bounded away from the yard, disappearing out of view down a long path.

'Oh, no!' said one of the men. 'We'll never catch the little devil now.'

Then he started arguing with the other man about whose fault it was that the goat had escaped, and the woman burst into tears.

'Don't panic,' Rory said. 'He'll be somewhere on the farm. We'll find him.' He started limping off after the goat.

'What's going on?' Darren turned to see his dad at the barn door.

'Big emergency, Dad,' Darren said. 'Got to go! See you later.'

He couldn't bear to stay in the barn and listen to his parents talking about him as they went through all the paperwork. Instead, he ran down the path after Rory.

The path led down to a pond, with a tall tree leaning over it. Rory was standing by the tree, rubbing his leg. When he saw Darren, he smiled. 'All right, lad? Come to join the chase?'

Darren nodded.

Rory slapped him on the back. 'Great stuff.' He

leaned in towards Darren. 'Tell you the truth, I'm not really up to running any more. My legs aren't as young as they used to be. And that little fella goes like lightning.'

'Which way did he go?' Darren asked.

'Straight on down.' Rory pointed further along the path. 'He's heading for the fields. There's some other goats down there. He might go and join them. But there's the vegetable garden too – if he's hungry, he'll go after the carrots and radishes. I'll check there.'

'OK,' Darren said. 'I'll see if I can find him.'

'Good luck,' Rory said, with a grin. 'I think you might need it!' He limped off towards a gate that led into a vegetable patch. Darren could see bean plants with bright-red flowers climbing up wigwams made of sticks, and underneath them a couple of marrows like big sausage-shaped balloons.

Darren ran on down the path to the fields, dodging through the visitors. Some of them were admiring a bright orange pig that had a big enclosure all to itself. The pig was trundling a football around, but Darren didn't stop to look.

Soon he came to an open area, with grassy paddocks fenced off. These must be the fields that Rory had mentioned. Darren walked closer. Now he could see a group of goats in one of the smaller paddocks, but there was no sign of a black and white one with them.

He went up to the biggest field. A horse and a pony and a furry donkey were standing with their ears pricked, staring towards an open shed at the top of the field.

The donkey saw Darren. Then he turned back to gaze up at the shed and opened his jaws to make a wheezy, rasping noise.

'Ee-yore!' he went.

'What's up?' Darren asked.

The donkey rolled his eyes in a comical way. He looked uneasy, and so did the horses. There must be something going on in the shed. Darren climbed over the fence, a bit scared that the horse might follow him. He'd never been up close to a horse before. But it didn't – they all just stayed where they were, looking anxiously at the shed.

Darren approached the shed cautiously and peered inside.

'Meh-eh-eh!'

There was the little goat, lying on a pile of straw and chewing a massive carrot. He must have got into the vegetable garden and stolen it.

'Hello, mate!' Darren said, squatting down.

The goat blinked at him and carried on eating.

'Fancy taking a walk back up to the farmyard?' Darren reached out to stroke the goat.

The goat dropped the carrot, sprang to his feet and dived towards Darren, trying to dodge past him and run out of the shed.

'Whoa!' Darren gasped. He flung himself sideways in a perfect rugby tackle. Mr Jefford, the school rugby coach, would have been really proud of him, Darren thought, as he threw his arms round the little goat and brought him down.

Now they were both lying in the straw. Darren sat up, holding onto his little captive.

'Meh-eh-eh!' said the goat, and tried to head-butt him in the chest.

'Hey! Steady!' Darren laughed. 'Watch it, or I'll do that right back to you.'

He pushed his head against the goat's forehead, just to show that he meant what he said.

The little animal didn't seem to mind. He leaned his face against Darren's, almost as if he was saying 'Hello' in a goat sort of way.

Now they were so close to each other Darren could see right into the goat's golden eyes. They were amazing, quite different to any other eyes he'd ever seen. The pupil wasn't round, like a human's. It was a long, horizontal line across the middle of the iris. Like a devil's eye, in a comic book.

'Wow, mate,' he said to the goat. 'You're cool.'

He wrapped both arms tightly round the animal and somehow managed to stand up without letting go of it, though the goat wriggled like anything.

'OK, bro! Let's head back.'

As Darren walked across the field, the horse and pony and donkey gazed at him in astonishment. Hadn't they ever seen a boy carrying a goat before? Darren grinned and hurried on towards the path.

He had to get his new friend back up to the farmyard before he escaped again.

Chapter Three

Rory was sitting on a bench by the pond, with his trouser legs rolled up to the knee. He was talking to some children who were feeding the ducks.

His white eyebrows shot up in surprise when he saw Darren with the goat in his arms.

'Well done!' he said. 'Where was he? And how did you catch him?'

Darren explained about the shed and the rugby tackle.

'I didn't hurt him though. I just tripped him up. We both fell over in the straw.'

'Good work.' Rory nodded in approval.

Darren gripped the goat's legs tightly. Several times on the way up the path, the little animal had wriggled so hard he'd almost dropped him.

'Well done for keeping hold of him. He's very strong, for such a little fellow,' Rory added, looking down ruefully at the bruise on his shin. He pulled a piece of rope out of his pocket and tied a loop in the end of it. Then he checked that the loop held firm and didn't pull any tighter. 'We don't want to strangle you, young fella-me-lad!' he said to the goat, as he slipped the loop over his head and gave the end of the rope to Darren. 'Especially now you'll be staying with us longer than planned.'

'What do you mean?' Darren asked.

'Did you see the lady who brought him?'

'The one who was crying?'

Rory nodded. 'Turns out she's having real problems keeping him under control – she's at her wits end. So I said we'd keep him on after the show; give him a home.'

'Oh.'

'You can put him down now and lead him. Watch he doesn't make another bid for freedom.'

The goat seemed quite calm. He trotted happily beside Darren and Rory as they made their way up to the farmyard.

'What's his name?' Darren asked.

'Don't know yet,' Rory said, 'It might be "Billy",

since he's a boy goat – though we've already got one goat with that name! We'll soon find out.'

When they got back to the farmyard the goat's old owner was very pleased to see that he was safe.

'You've broken the record for catching him,' she said to Darren. 'Usually it takes all day. And at least four people.'

'He'll be fine here,' Rory said with a smile.

Darren felt his face grow warm. It seemed like he'd achieved something pretty special, though all he'd done was a bit of fast running and some rugby tactics.

'Thank you so much for taking him,' the lady said. 'Here's his paperwork.' She handed a folder to Rory.

Darren wondered if it contained any comments about the goat's antisocial behaviour, like there were in his file.

'He's a very good example of the breed,' the lady was saying now. 'And pygmy goats are very popular with kids.'

'Hmm, yes.' Rory looked doubtful. 'We might have to do some training with him before we can trust him with small children.'

'Yes, of course!' the lady replied, opening the car door. The two men were already inside, waiting to leave. 'Thanks again. Have a marvellous show.'

The car and trailer drove out of the farm gate and away up the road.

Rory wiped his forehead as he watched them go. 'I hope all our rare-breed visitors aren't such a handful as this one.'

'He's being good now,' Darren said, scratching the tufts of hair that grew between the goat's horns. 'Why d'you have to have all these other animals anyway? Haven't you got enough?'

Rory nodded. 'We get visitors – families and school kids and all sorts of folk – who come back week after week to see the animals. Like Cynthia, our Tamworth sow.'

'The big ginger one?' Darren said, remembering the pig with the football.

'That's right. Everybody knows her. So we thought we'd invite some other unusual farm animals along. That way, more visitors will come and see them. We've even got a bull arriving today.'

'Wow,' Darren said. Maybe his two weeks at the farm would be more interesting than he thought. He'd never seen a bull before, but it sounded pretty exciting.

Rory smiled at him. 'I'm glad you've turned up, Darren. You're going to be a real help with getting the show together. Right, let's get this fellow sorted out.'

Rory opened up the folder. Darren noticed his face fall as he began to read. Had the little goat had done something really naughty? Darren wouldn't be at all surprised if he had.

Rory shook his head, staring down at the folder. '"Beech Tree Farm Prince Balthazar".'

'What?' Darren laughed.

'That's his name,' Rory said. 'Maybe we could just call him "Prince".'

Darren looked down at the goat. He'd got bored of standing quietly and was chewing on the laces of Darren's trainers.

'I don't know. "Prince" is OK, but it doesn't sound quite right.'

'Meh-eh!' said the goat, as if he was agreeing with him. He spun round and butted him on the leg.

'Ouch!' Darren gasped. 'Give over, mate!'

Rory laughed. 'Sorry, but that was hilarious. I'm glad I'm not the only one he wants to bash up.'

Darren grinned. 'I've got it,' he said. 'Basher.'

'Perfect!' Rory said with a grin. 'Even sounds a bit like Balthazar, though it's a much better name for this little fella.'

'How's it going?' Darren's dad called over. He and

Darren's mum were coming out of the barn.

'Fine,' Rory said, dodging out of the way as Basher tried to get his leg again. 'Your lad's certainly got a way with goats.'

Darren's mum beamed. 'He'll get that from me,' she said. 'We had some lovely goats when I was a girl. Dear little white ones. I used to play such games with them—'

'OK, Mum,' Darren interrupted. Once she got going on one of her tales about her childhood in Ireland, there would be no stopping her. But he couldn't help feeling a warm glow inside, as he thought about what Rory had just said. It seemed ages since anyone had said anything nice about him.

'You'll be all right, then?' Dad said. He didn't look quite so angry now.

'Yup.' Darren held Basher's rope very tight, so he wouldn't start anything. 'See you later.'

His parents walked off through the gate and set off on their way home to the flats. They were holding hands. Darren felt a bit sad as he watched them. They hardly ever spent any time together, what with his dad working days and his mum on the night shift. Going to work, sleeping, shopping, doing the housework – and nagging him: that's all they ever seemed to do.

'Now then,' Rory said, 'here's two young 'uns who're waiting to meet you.'

Darren saw two kids approaching: the sandy-haired boy he'd met earlier, and an Asian girl with a thin face. She was wearing a blue headscarf, and was carrying a big shoulder bag.

'Hi,' she said shyly. 'I'm Asha, and this is Jack. We're just going to the café. D'you want to come too?'

Darren would've much rather stayed with Basher, but Rory took the rope from him.

'Leave this little madcap to me, and go and get yourself some elevenses. I should think you're ready for them after all that rushing around,' he said.

So Darren had to follow the two kids into the café, which was next to the barn. The three of them got juice and doughnuts from the counter and then went to join Kerry, who was sitting at one of the tables drinking coffee.

'Hey, Asha,' she said, as soon as they sat down. 'Having a better day today?'

'Not really,' Asha said. She sighed. 'I just can't get it right.'

Darren wondered what they were talking about.

'Let's see what you've done,' said Jack. 'That picture of Cynthia that you showed me yesterday was ace.'

'It wasn't Cynthia,' the girl said. 'It was meant to be Dusty.'

Jack bit his lip. 'Sorry,' he said.

The girl got a drawing out of her bag and laid it on the table. Darren stared at it. It was obviously an animal, but he couldn't work out what kind of animal.

'I tried to draw Dusty again from memory. But I just can't do it.' Asha sighed and took a bite of her doughnut.

Darren studied the drawing. It looked like a blob with four legs – a bit like a toy made out of twisted balloons that he'd been given at a birthday party once, when he was very little.

'Who's Dusty?' he asked.

'He's the donkey,' Asha replied. 'I've tried drawing him from life too, but that didn't work either. First he got tangled up in the tree and then he ran away! I'm just no good at art. I really can't draw.'

'Anyone can draw,' Darren said. 'It's easy, if you know how.'

Kerry looked at him for a moment. Then she pulled a piece of blank paper out of Asha's bag. 'Why don't you show us, Darren?' She pushed the paper towards him.

Darren's face went hot. Why hadn't he kept his

mouth shut?

Asha was staring at him with big brown eyes. 'Oh, please.' She looked away as if she was embarrassed. 'I mean, only if you want to?'

Darren fumbled in his pocket for one of his felt-tips. 'OK,' he muttered.

He closed his eyes for a moment, remembering the donkey in the field, with his big head, thin neck, and long furry ears. Then he began to draw.

'Everything is made up of shapes,' he said, sketching two rectangles on the paper - a big one for Dusty's head and a long, thin one for his neck. 'You break the animal down into those shapes. One at a time. And then you add the detail.'

Darren added a half-closed eye to the first rectangle he'd drawn, and then a pair of floppy ears.

'Oh, my gosh!' Asha squealed. 'It's Dusty!'

'Shhh,' Jack whispered. 'Don't disturb him.'

But nothing would have interrupted Darren now. He was completely lost in another zone – the place he always went to when he was working on his art.

He added a straggly mane along the top of the donkey's neck, and began work on a third rectangle for the body. He drew the short legs with their round hooves and knobbly knees, and finally added the tail.

'Wow!' Asha gasped.

Darren finished sketching in the tassel on the end of Dusty's tail and looked up. Asha, Kerry and Jack were staring at the drawing with their mouths open, and everyone else in the café was hurrying over to see too.

Darren drew a speech balloon coming out of the donkey's mouth, and added: *Ee-yore!* in bubble-style graffiti lettering.

'Awesome,' Jack sighed.

Darren was just going to explain some more about how he'd used shapes to bring Dusty to life in the drawing, when Rory came rushing through the café door.

'Darren, I need your help with young fella-me-lad,' he said, slightly out of breath. 'Can you come and see if you can work your magic with our new guest. He won't stop bashing everything in sight!'

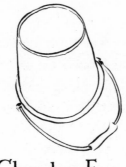

Chapter Four

'Here he is,' Rory said, opening the gate to one of the pens in the farmyard.

'He's *gorgeous*!' Asha whispered.

She was so pleased she'd asked Rory if she could come along. She'd never seen such a cute baby goat. He was so perfect with his black and white patches, his shiny hooves and his little pointed horns. She just wanted to cuddle him.

As she reached out to pick him up, Basher jumped in the air and ran away, hiding behind a hay bale.

'What did I do?' Asha felt a bit hurt. She'd only been going to pet him.

The new boy, Darren, came into the pen. 'He's winding you up,' he said. 'Hey, Basher!' He climbed onto the hay bale and reached down to scratch the little goat's head.

Asha tried really hard not to be scared as Darren walked past her, but her insides felt tight, the way they always did when she walked through the estate where she lived, and the older boys were hanging about. She recognized Darren now. He was one of them. She'd seen him and his friends lots of times.

'Don't worry, lass,' Rory said. 'He's still very young, is Basher. He's trying to play with you, like he would with another baby goat.'

'Kid, you mean!' Asha said.

Rory chuckled. 'That's right. Baby goats, baby humans. Both known as "kids". And both very naughty, sometimes.'

'Go, Basher!' Darren laughed, as the little goat jumped up onto the hay bale with him and tried to head-butt his leg.

'See, Asha. He's just playing,' Rory said. 'Trouble is, he can be a bit rough. And he's so cute that all the children who come to visit will want to pet him. So it would be great if you and Darren could work with him – give him some training and get him to settle down and be more gentle.'

'How?' Asha asked, her stomach churning at the thought of having to work with Darren.

'The best way is to reward him when he's good, and ignore him when he does something you don't like,' Rory explained. 'That way, he'll be keen to try and please you.' He pulled a bag of treats – chunks of carrot and apple – out of his pocket. 'You can use these as a reward. Tell him he's a good boy, and give him a treat. He'll be the best-behaved goat on the farm in no time.'

'OK.' Asha took the bag of treats.

'You can always scratch him between the front legs too. That'll calm him down.'

'Of course!' Asha remembered the way the other goats stood still and let their heads hang down when she did that to them.

A horn started honking loudly outside the City Farm gates.

'Got to dash,' Rory said. 'I'm expecting a couple of Manx Longhorn lambs. That'll be them, I should think.' And he hurried away.

Now Asha was alone with Darren. He was sitting on the hay bale with his chin in his hands, looking around the goat pen.

He was so much bigger than her, and seemed so much older. She couldn't help remembering how much she hated walking past him and his friends.

But he'd only just arrived at the Harvest Hope project and Asha knew it was her job to talk to him, and make him feel at home.

'Your drawing was brilliant,' she said. 'It looked exactly like Dusty.'

'Thanks.' Darren shrugged his shoulders and his face went a bit pink.

'Can you draw other animals too?'

''Course!' Darren said. 'I'll do some others, later, if you want.'

'You must be a genius at art.'

'I'm all right.' Darren went really red. 'It's the only thing I'm any good at.'

'You're lucky,' Asha said. 'I'm not good at anything. Except talking.'

Darren laughed, and Asha thought how different he looked when he was smiling. Much friendlier.

'So I won't mind if you tell me to shut up,' she continued.

Darren shrugged again. 'Why would I?' he said. 'Shall we get on with what he said? Doing the training?'

Asha nodded. 'What shall we do?'

Basher was lying down now next to Darren on the hay bale, and nibbling at his jeans.

'He likes jumping. Let's try and get him to jump

when we want him to,' Darren said.

He got up from the hay bale. Basher quickly followed him.

Asha got a chunk of apple, and went round to the other side of the hay bale. She held the treat high in the air.

'Up, Basher!' she said.

'Meh-eh-eh!' Basher answered, and leaped straight onto the bale.

'Yay!' Asha was thrilled. She gave him his reward.

Darren grinned. 'Wicked,' he said. 'You're a really cool trainer, Asha.'

They tried this trick again a few times. Basher very quickly got the idea. Soon, he didn't even need a treat to encourage him. All they had to do was call out 'Up!' and he would leap onto the bale and wait for their applause.

'Tell you what,' Darren said. 'We could get him to be like a circus goat.'

'What d'you mean?'

'Well – when I was a kid my mum once took me to the circus, and we saw a goat that rode on a horse's back.'

'We'd have to train the horse to stand still,' Asha said. 'That might take a long time.'

'We could try this.' Darren got down on all fours in the straw, and made his back flat, so it was like a table.

Asha grinned. 'Up, Basher!' she called.

The goat jumped onto Darren's back and posed there, his head held high.

'Yay!' Asha cried, clapping loudly. 'You should do that in the show.'

'Ouch!' Darren winced. 'His hooves are really sharp.'

'Oh, no! Down, Basher.' Asha held out a chunk of carrot, and the little goat leaped off Darren's back and trotted over to take it from her fingers. 'What a shame. That would've been the best thing in the show…'

Darren thought for a moment. 'No problem. I can wear my body warmer. That'll protect me. I'll bring it next time.'

'Brilliant!' Asha sighed with relief.

'Hey, I think I deserve a reward after that,' Darren said. 'Give us some of that apple.'

'It's gone a bit brown,' Asha said, peering into the bag. 'Do you want a mint instead?' She always kept a pack of mints in her pocket. They were a favourite treat for the horses, sheep and goats.

'Cheers.' Darren took a mint and sat on the haybale. 'So, where d'you live, then?'

Asha took a deep breath. She'd been having so much fun she'd forgotten to be scared of Darren. 'On the estate,' she muttered. 'In the block of flats near the shops.'

Darren frowned. 'That's weird. That's where I live, but I've never seen you before.'

'I've been ill. I had leukaemia and I was in hospital for ages,' Asha said. 'Even when I came home I didn't feel like going out much. I just lay on the sofa all the time.'

'That's really bad.' Darren looked shocked. 'Is that why you wear a scarf? 'Cos of the chemo? My auntie had that and all her hair fell out. She's OK now though.'

Asha nodded. 'I'm OK now too. Shall we try some more tricks?'

Darren nodded and grinned. 'Let's make an obstacle course!'

The two of them found some more hay bales and stacked them up in a small tower. Darren got a bucket and turned it upside down for Basher to stand and pose on. Then he laid some poles out to make a jump.

At first the little goat didn't understand what they wanted. He knocked the bucket over and nibbled at the hay. And he wouldn't jump over the poles.

'I know,' Asha said. 'He's really good at following. I'll get him to run after me.' She got a mint out of her pocket and waved it under Basher's nose. Then she set off round the obstacle course. She leaped over the poles, balanced on the bucket and scrambled up the tower.

'Go, Basher!' Darren called.

Basher trotted round after Asha. He didn't quite get everything right the first time, but after three circuits he'd got the idea, and could do everything perfectly.

'Phew!' Asha leaned against the hay bale tower. She was feeling really tired. 'How was that?'

'Wicked,' Darren answered. Then he looked at her anxiously. 'You all right?'

'I'm OK!' Asha said, but she was still panting from all the dashing around.

'Hey! Sit down, have a rest. You shouldn't have run about like that.' Darren dragged a hay bale down from the tower to make a seat.

'I wanted to. It was fun. I'll be all right – in a minute.'

Asha sat down on the bale, and Darren sat next to her. Basher trotted over to them.

'His eyes are weird, aren't they?' Darren said, scratching the goat's head. 'The way the pupil goes across in a line like that.'

Asha nodded. 'That's what I thought the first time I saw the other goats here. Rory explained why they're like that – it's amazing.'

'Why?' Darren asked.

'It's 'cos wild goats need to look out for predators creeping up on them over the plains. Lions, and things like that. So their pupil goes across like that to help them focus on a wide area. Horses' eyes work the same way. And sheep's too.'

'Wow. I'd never have thought of that.' Darren looked at Basher and smiled.

'And our human eyes are like they are because we need to focus close up much more,' Asha said, proud that she'd remembered Rory's explanation.

The little goat put his nose up to sniff at Darren's face.

'He loves you!' Asha said with a giggle.

Darren looked embarrassed. 'Hey, get off!' He pushed Basher away.

'It's OK. He can smell the mint on your breath, that's all. The other goats are just as bad.'

Asha couldn't help smiling as she gave Basher another minty treat. She was pretty sure though that the little goat did like Darren – a lot. He was lying next to his feet now, snuggling up against his leg.

And Darren was nothing like as scary as she'd thought. He'd turned out to be a kind and thoughtful person, and really good fun too.

It was going to be great having him at the farm for the next fortnight.

Chapter Five

Darren looked out of his bedroom window. It was ages since he'd eaten his dinner, but the sky was only just turning pink above the block of flats across the courtyard.

His mum had left for work about an hour ago. She'd asked him endless questions about the farm, and she was thrilled that he'd made friends with a goat. She knew Asha too.

'Poor wee girl,' she'd said. 'Her dad has the newsagents, down on the parade. I'm glad she's better from her leukaemia.'

Now everything was peaceful in the flat. Dad was sprawled on the living-room sofa in front of the TV. And Darren was doing his favourite thing in the whole world: drawing.

He'd saved up to buy a big sketchbook, with thick white pages and a shiny black cover. He'd especially wanted a black one, because that's what all the famous graffiti artists had. They called their sketchbooks 'black books'.

Now he was jotting down some ideas for Asha's posters. He drew loads of action outlines of Basher, jumping high in the air. The little goat did the most amazing turns when he leaped, twisting his body into an 'S' shape.

Next, he did a few close-up sketches of Basher's face, with his big eyes, pointed beard and swept-back horns.

Then Darren tried to think of a background. He remembered what his mum had said that morning, about the barn looking like an old mother hen. He tried out a couple of graffiti-style versions of this. They looked brilliant. The barn really came to life when he made its long walls into wings, and the door and windows into a beak and eyes.

The doorbell to his flat gave a shrill warble. Darren jumped with shock. He'd been miles away. Voices sounded in the hall. It was Gary and Steven, his classmates from school.

Dad knocked on the bedroom door, then stuck his

head round. 'Your friends have come to call for you,' he said. 'Don't be late back, if you go out.' Then he yawned and headed back to the sofa. He'd probably be asleep very soon, and wouldn't notice what time Darren got home.

'Right-oh, Dad,' Darren called, as Gary and Steven pushed through the bedroom door, elbowing each other to be first.

'Doodling again?' Gary asked, leaning over to look at the drawings.

'Just a few animal sketches.' Darren closed the sketchbook and shoved it under his bed, right at the back. He used to hide his spray cans there, but they'd been confiscated, after he was caught graffitiing the school.

'Animals? How boring is that?' Steven snorted.

Steven was thirteen, the same age as Darren and Gary, but he wasn't as tall as them. He still looked like a little kid, but he was brilliant at riding his BMX bike.

The bike was in the hall now, leaning up against the wall. Steven had brought it up with him in the lift, to keep it safe.

'Wanna go out?' Gary asked. 'Or shall we go on your Xbox?'

Darren's Xbox was in the living room, next to the

big new TV. He wasn't allowed to play on it in his bedroom. But Dad wouldn't exactly welcome the three of them Xbox-ing tonight, while he was trying to sleep on the sofa.

'Out,' Darren said.

Half of him wanted to tell the other two to go without him, so he could stay and carry on with his drawings. It would be fantastic if he could go back to the farm tomorrow with some great designs for Asha's posters. But the other half of him was glad to get away from the flat and be heading out for some fresh air.

Not that the air was particularly fresh, where the three of them ended up hanging out, down by the bins that belonged to the parade of shops. The hot weather made the rubbish in the bins smell rank: of mouldy fruit and rotten fish.

Steven circled on his bike and did a few wheelies. Darren got a felt-tip out and did a quick sketch of him on a notice that was pasted to the side of one of the bins.

'I'm bored out of my brain,' Gary moaned, kicking the side of the bin and making a loud booming noise. 'There's nothing to do in this place. Let's go back and go on the Xbox.'

Darren shook his head. 'We can't. Dad'll go mental.'

Gary sighed and kicked the bin again. 'Have you got your cans with you?'

'Nah,' Darren said. 'My dad confiscated them.'

'Boring!' Gary said, kicking the bin again. Then he looked round and picked up a broken bottle that was lying by the bottom of the bins. Darren didn't know what he had in mind, but he didn't like Gary's expression.

'Don't, Gazza,' he said, looking over his shoulder.

There was no one about. Half the shops on the parade were closed down, with metal shutters fixed over their windows. And right now, on this hot evening, no one was using the launderette, or buying anything from the greengrocers or the newsagents.

'S'all right,' Gary said. 'Stay cool.'

He held the bottle by the neck and scraped the broken end against one of the bins, making a horrible noise. He started scratching out some letters.

THIS BIN STINKS, Gary wrote.

Darren couldn't help laughing. It was true – the bin smelled disgusting. But then he heard footsteps coming from one of the shops. He looked up and saw a tall, thin, Asian man and a girl wearing a blue headscarf. It was Asha. Darren caught his breath.

'Gazza, stop,' he hissed. 'Someone's seen you.'

Gary chucked the bottle against the wall. It broke, with a crash. Then he ran off towards the park. Steven had already disappeared, pedalling like crazy in the direction of the block where he lived.

Darren's heart was beating so hard it felt like a rabbit was kicking him inside his chest. Asha had seen him. She was looking right at him. The man beside her – who must be her father, because Darren had seen him behind the counter in the newsagents – was pulling her hand, trying to lead her away from the bins.

But Asha carried on staring at Darren. Any minute now, she'd call his name. He slouched back against the bins, looking down at the ground as if he hadn't noticed her. His face felt burning hot. What must she have thought, when she saw Gary throwing the bottle?

Darren looked around quickly, pretending he'd heard someone calling his name in the park. Then he ran after Gary, as fast as he could. He didn't look back to see if Asha was still watching him. But he knew she would be.

Chapter Six

'You're very quiet,' Kerry said, next morning, when Asha arrived at the barn. 'Is anything wrong?'

Asha shook her head.

'Flapjack?' Kerry held out a plate.

Normally flapjacks were Asha's favourite snack. But she didn't fancy one right now. She was so nervous about seeing Darren this morning that she felt really sick.

When she'd first noticed him last night, by the bins, she'd wanted to wave and shout his name. She'd really wanted to introduce him to her dad. But then she'd seen the other two boys. And the skinny one had smashed a bottle against the wall.

'Let's go,' her dad had said. 'Those boys are trouble, Asha.'

Darren had seen her. He'd looked right at her. And then he'd just run away, following the skinny boy into the park.

Asha had tried to explain that he was a friend of hers – from the farm.

'Up to no good,' her father said. 'Boys like that – it's best to have nothing to do with them. Let's go home now.' He'd squeezed Asha's hand. 'You must be careful. I can't always be with you when you walk through the estate.'

'Yes, Dad.'

Asha's heart had been pounding as she followed her dad up the stairway to the flat where they lived. Now she felt cold and scared as she remembered last night. How could Darren have ignored her like that? Her father was right. He must be no good.

She didn't want to talk about what had happened, so she went to sit on the sofa so that Kerry wouldn't ask any more questions. She opened her bag and got out a few of her drawings and pretended to look at them.

The barn door opened and Asha's heart turned a somersault. But it was only Jack.

'Hi, Asha!'

'Hi!' she replied. It was great to see Jack's friendly,

65

familiar face.

'Are you training the goat again today?' he asked, coming to sit beside her.

She shook her head. 'I thought I'd come and help you with Cynthia.'

'That'll be great,' Jack said with a wide grin. 'You'll be amazed how good she is at football now. We can play two humans against one pig.'

'Let's go!' Asha jumped to her feet and ran to the door. The quicker they got away from the barn, the less likely it was that she would have to see Darren.

'Hang on,' Kerry called. 'What about these?' She waved Asha's drawings at her. 'We need our posters! The show's at the end of next week.'

Asha was just about to say that she'd come back later, and, anyway, wasn't it just as important to work on training Cynthia so that she would be the ultimate superstar pig footballer? But then she saw Darren coming through the door, carrying a big black sketchbook under his arm.

It was too late to escape.

'Hi there, Darren! You're just in time to save the day,' said Kerry in a friendly voice. 'Asha needs your help with the posters.'

Asha's heart sank like a stone. Darren looked really

moody. He didn't say anything, just stared down at his trainers.

A chill ran through her body. Darren had seemed like a great person yesterday, when they'd been training Basher. He'd been kind, and fun to be with too. But he must have just been pretending. The real Darren was one of the gang who hung out on the estate. She knew that now. And he knew that she knew. He wouldn't be able to pretend with her any more.

Kerry was pulling two chairs to the big table where visiting kids could work on their projects when they came to the farm.

'There you go,' she said, flashing a smile at Darren. 'You'll need lots of room, to lay everything out.'

'Thanks,' Darren mumbled. He put his sketchbook down. Then he looked sideways at Kerry, and gave a little smile back.

It's just a fake, Asha thought. *Kerry doesn't know who he really is…*

But then Kerry and Jack went off and the two of them were alone together, sitting at the table. Neither of them spoke.

Asha looked down at the table, gripping her hands together tightly so that he couldn't see they were shaking. Her stupid drawing of Dusty was lying right in front of her, and she had to keep staring at it, even though she hated it. She didn't dare meet Darren's eyes.

He was shuffling through the pages of his sketchbook. After a few moments, he said: 'I did some drawings for you, yesterday.'

His voice sounded gruff; not the usual way he spoke at all. Asha nodded. She didn't know what else to do. She knew her voice would be all shaky if she said anything, and she didn't want to speak to him anyway.

Darren pushed the sketchbook across the table. 'Want to have a look?'

'Oh!' Asha caught her breath with surprise. There was Basher! His cute black and white face, exactly how he looked in real life.

'That's the first one I did,' Darren said. He reached over the table and turned the page. 'Then I worked it up a bit. Made him a bit more grafitti-style.'

The second drawing was so brilliant Asha couldn't help smiling. Basher looked really cheeky, as if he was about to leap off the page and do one of his naughty head-butts.

'Or,' Darren turned the page again, 'what about this?'

Asha burst out laughing. In the third drawing,

Basher was wearing shades. He looked so funny, like a little kid who was trying to be really cool.

Darren cleared his throat. 'What d'you think?' he asked.

'They're amazing!' Asha said, before she could stop herself.

'Great!' she heard Darren say.

Asha took a deep breath and looked up at him. He was watching her across the table. His mouth looked twisty, like he wanted to smile but wasn't sure if he should.

'Did you really do these yesterday?' she asked.

He nodded, and his face turned pink. 'Yup. When I got home.'

They both fell silent again. Now Darren looked down at the table. He pulled a pen out of his pocket and started doodling on a corner of the sketchpad.

Asha knew that if she didn't ask him right now what he was doing last night, she would never be able to.

'I saw you,' she said, and felt her cheeks going really hot. 'When I was coming back from the shops with my dad.'

'Yup,' he said. His voice had gone gruff again. 'I was going to come over and say hi, but I was a bit busy.'

He carried on doodling. Asha knew that he didn't want to talk about it, but she'd started now, and she couldn't stop herself.

'Busy? What d'you mean?'

'You know. With my mates. We were hanging out.'

'Your friend threw a bottle.'

Darren shrugged and looked down at the table. 'So? It was broken anyway.'

'But there were bits of glass everywhere, after he threw it. That's dangerous. There's lots of babies and toddlers on the estate. And animals too – dogs and cats. And the wild foxes. They could get hurt…' Asha's tongue was running away with her, like it often did. She tried really hard to stop talking.

Darren's frowned. 'It wasn't me who threw it, all right?'

'And your friend was scratching words on the bin, with that bottle…'

Darren slammed his sketchbook shut. 'Asha! Get off my back. It's none of your business what me and my mates do, OK?'

Asha felt suddenly angry. Why should he think that he had the right to do whatever he wanted? She lived on the estate too. So did lots of other people who never did anything wrong, or harmed anything or anybody.

'But you're destroying things on the estate. *Vandalizing...*' she said.

'I said, get off my back!' Darren shouted, jumping up from his chair. His face was very red.

Asha's heart leaped with fear. She looked across to the office, but Kerry wasn't there. She must have been out doing something on the farm. The barn was empty except for the two of them.

'Sorry,' Darren said in a quieter voice. 'I don't mean to yell at you. I just hate that word. *Vandalize.*'

Asha's heart was still racing. But at least Darren wasn't shouting any more.

'Why d'you do it?' she asked him. 'Why spoil everything and make the estate look horrible?'

Darren sat down again. He sighed. 'What else is there to do in that dump?'

'What dump?'

'That stupid estate. There's nowhere to go, and nothing to do. You live there too, Asha – don't you ever get bored?'

Asha shook her head. 'No. I don't. You mean you break things because you're bored?'

'Yeah. We're bored out of our brains, most of the time, me and my mates. Last night, right – we couldn't stay in, because my dad was having a sleep in the living room. And my bedroom's too small for three of us to sit in. Where can we go except round the estate? And there's nothing to do. It's just boring.' He leaned his head in his hands, looking really miserable.

Asha thought for a moment. 'I know what it's like, being bored,' she said.

Darren shrugged, as if he didn't believe her.

Asha carried on talking. 'When I was having my treatment, I had to stay in hospital. I was there for months and months.'

Darren looked up. 'Couldn't you watch telly?'

'No.' Asha shivered, as she remembered how sick she'd felt when she was having her chemotherapy. 'They brought me one, but it just made my head ache, so I told them to take it away. And where my bed was I couldn't even see out of the window.'

'So what did you do? Read a book?'

'My eyes went funny if I tried to. I just lay there.'

Darren stared at her. 'That's bad.'

Asha nodded. 'The nurses were really kind, but they were too busy to come and talk to me. Mum and Dad had to work, and look after my little brother and sister too, so they could only come in for a little while in the evening.'

'I'd have gone crazy,' Darren said.

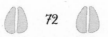

'I think I did, a bit,' Asha said. 'I used to look at the clock on the wall and it seemed like the minute hand was stuck, and time would never move on. I thought I'd just be lying there for ever. It made me want to scream.'

'Why didn't you?'

'I couldn't!' Asha exclaimed. 'There were other kids in the ward who were just as poorly as me. Some of them were even more ill. I would've frightened them.'

Darren frowned and looked down at his sketchpad. He opened it and started doodling again.

'But you know what – it was a good thing for me, in the end,' Asha said, after a moment.

'How?'

'I'll never, ever be bored again,' Asha explained. 'Even when I'm not doing anything – just sitting in the living room at home, hearing Mum making tea in the kitchen, and watching the clouds go by and the birds coming to our balcony to eat the peanuts – all that seems really interesting now.'

Darren looked at her like she was crazy. 'You're kidding. Really?'

'Yup!' Asha grinned. 'And now that I can come to the farm, I'm not bored for a single minute. There's always something happening…'

Right on cue, the barn door burst upon, and Jack raced in, his face bright red from running.

'Basher's got out!' he gasped. 'He's running like crazy. I tried to catch him, but he's too fast!'

'See what I mean?' Asha said, but Darren was already on his feet and hurrying out into the farmyard.

Chapter Seven

'Have you seen a goat?' Darren called to a boy who was standing in the farmyard.

The boy nodded. 'A small black and white one just headed that way,' he said, pointing down the path. 'You'll have to be really fast to catch him though.'

'No worries!' Darren raced on, closely followed by Jack and Asha.

There was no sign of Basher in the garden. Maybe he'd gone back to the horses' field. The three of them hurried on.

A crowd of people were standing round the pond. They were all looking up into the branches of the tree that stood next to it.

'Oh, no! Look where he is!' Asha cried. 'We'll never get him down from there!'

Basher had somehow managed to jump up onto one of the branches of the tree. He was posing there with his head high and his eyes shining.

'He must have got onto the bench and then leaped up,' Darren said. He couldn't help feeling proud of the little goat. Basher really was amazing – he wasn't afraid of anything. But it was going to be very tricky getting him down.

'I could climb up and grab him,' Jack suggested. 'It might be easier for me, 'cos I'm not as tall as you.'

'Good idea,' Darren said.

Jack was right. The branch was quite narrow, and there were other branches just above it. It would be a tight squeeze for Darren to climb up there. But it was still a tricky manoeuvre – even for Jack.

'Mind he doesn't head-butt you!' Darren called, as Jack clambered up the tree.

'Stand underneath, Darren, in case they fall,' Asha called, her eyes wide with tension.

Jack was now sitting on the branch with his legs hanging down on either side. Darren crouched on the bench below.

'Steady, Basher,' Jack said, inching forward along the branch.

'Meh-eh-eh!' Basher replied, blinking in a friendly way.

One or two of the people watching called out encouraging words.

Darren held his breath. Jack was almost there now.

'How can I get hold of him?' he called down. 'It would be much easier if he had a collar on, like our other goats...'

Before Darren could say anything, Basher sprang off the branch, leaping high in the air like a gymnast on a trampoline.

'No!' Darren yelled, shutting his eyes tightly.

He couldn't bear to see what happened next. It was a long way down to the ground. No way could the little goat land without hurting himself.

Next thing, Darren heard a huge splash, and a loud 'Oooh!' of shock from the people standing nearby. He opened his eyes to see a trail of bubbles in the middle of the pond.

Basher had jumped so far that he was well clear of the ground that surrounded the tree. He'd hit the surface of the pond and disappeared under the water.

Jack was still clinging to the tree. Asha looked up at Darren, her eyes huge with alarm.

'We've got to get him out!' she said, and headed for the pond.

'No, Asha. Not you,' Darren called after her. 'You

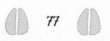

77

mustn't! Wait here.'

She was already up to her ankles in the water. But Darren couldn't let her go any further into the muddy pond – not when she was still recovering from her illness.

He ran past her, splashing through the water to where Basher had fallen in. The pond was quite deep, and in the middle the water was up to his waist. The bottom of it felt squishy under his feet, like there were all kinds of horrible things down there.

Darren was just holding his nose ready to put his head under and see where the goat was, when a huge cheer went up from the onlookers. Basher had surfaced.

His eyes were bulging with fright, and he was paddling wildly with his little legs to stay afloat, like a toddler learning to swim.

'It's OK, mate.' Darren reached out and slid his arm under Basher's belly. 'I've got you.'

He lifted the little goat out of the water and strode back to dry land. Basher looked terrible. His coat was sopping wet, and his white patches were all smeared brown with mud.

'Oh, my gosh!' Kerry came running down the path. 'What's happened? And why are you up in the tree, Jack?'

Asha explained how Basher had jumped up the tree, then into the pond and how Darren had rescued him.

'The little monster,' Kerry said, but she was smiling as she stroked Basher's head. 'You would decide to do that when we're having one of our busiest days ever!' Her smile grew bigger as she saw Jack scramble safely back down to ground level again.

'Shall we put Basher in one of the stables?' Asha suggested. 'He won't be able to jump out of there.'

'Great idea. Then we'll get Rory to make the fence round his enclosure a bit higher. That should keep him in. You can clean him up later. Right now, we need to sort Darren out.'

'I'm all right,' Darren said, looking down at his muddy jeans. 'I'll soon dry out.' It was weird, but getting dirty just seemed like part of being on the farm now. He didn't mind it at all.

Kerry shook her head. 'No, we've got plenty of clean things you can borrow,' she said. 'Your jeans will be ponging like anything in a little while with all that pond muck on them. And you need to have a good wash. You didn't put your head under the water, did you? Or swallow any of it?'

Darren shook his head and Kerry looked relieved.

'I'm sure the pond's fine – but it's best to be careful!' she said.

Kerry led the way back up to the farmyard. Darren's jeans were already a bit whiffy, where the hot sun was drying out the mud.

She found him a clean pair of trousers while he washed himself in the barn's bathroom. 'There you go!' she grinned, handing over the trousers when he came out. 'Now you can go off and get yourself all dirty again cleaning out an enclosure for the next arrival. Come on, follow me.'

Darren, Asha and Jack followed her out of the barn and over to a large pen on the far side of the farmyard.

'Who's that for?' Jack asked.

'The rare-breed bull's due to arrive at any minute,' Kerry explained. 'So his new home will need to be spick and span.'

Darren set to work sweeping up all the dirty straw from the floor of the enclosure, and forking it into a wheelbarrow. Asha scrubbed out the food manger, and got some pellets of cattle feed to put in it.

Jack brought two big buckets of clean water. 'He'll be thirsty after his journey,' he said.

They were only just finished in time. A lorry

rumbled through the gate and into the yard, and a man in a green jacket led a stocky, red-brown bull down the ramp at the back. The bull turned his head to look at everything, his little eyes bright under his wide forehead.

'Wow,' Asha said. 'He looks quite fierce.'

'He's an old sweetie,' the man said, scratching the bull's head. 'Treat him with respect and he won't give you no trouble, will you, Charlie?'

The bull lowered his head for more scratching.

'He's much smaller than my grandad's bull was, at Hilltop Farm,' Jack said.

'He's a Dexter bull, that's why,' the man explained. 'They're bred to be little. Ideal for a small city farm.'

Darren approached warily.

'You in charge, lad?' the man asked him. 'I see you've been getting his place ready for him.'

Darren felt his face go hot. 'Well, I—'

'Here, lead him in.' The man passed him the rope.

Darren hoped the others couldn't see that his knees were shaking as he walked into the enclosure with Charlie. But there was nothing to fear. The bull followed him quietly.

Then he smelled the food that Asha had put in the manger for him.

'He's really strong!' Darren said, as the bull pulled on the rope to get at the treats.

'He is. But he's kind too,' the man said. 'He won't mess about with you. Not if you treat him with respect.'

Charlie dropped his nose into the manger and began crunching up the food. Darren unclipped the rope and hurried out of the enclosure.

'Darren – that was brave!' Kerry said, coming across the farmyard. She stared at the bull with wide eyes. Then she shook hands with the man, and took the paperwork from him.

'"King Charles of Old Oak Farm",' she read. 'He'll look fantastic in the show's Grand Parade. Thanks ever so much for bringing him.'

No sooner had the cattle lorry departed than a car and trailer came trundling into the farmyard.

Kerry smiled. 'You're going to love these next ones, Asha,' she said.

'It's absolutely gorgeous. But what is it?' Asha asked, as Kerry led a long-legged creature with huge eyes and a curly coat out of the trailer.

'She's an alpaca,' Kerry explained. She held the alpaca at the bottom of the ramp and called up into the trailer: 'Come on, little one!'

With a patter of hooves, a baby alpaca raced down

the ramp and ran to lean against her mother's side.

'That's so cute!' Asha breathed.

'Meet Candy and her baby, Sugar,' Kerry said, smiling at Asha. 'We've got to take very good care of them.'

'You'd better take over,' Darren said, stepping back. He could tell that Asha had fallen in love with the alpacas.

Asha's face shone with delight as she took Candy's rope and led her and her tiny daughter to their pen.

The next arrivals came by car. The man who brought them lifted a large hamper out from the back seat.

'Where d'you want these?' he asked Darren.

Darren peered through a gap in the side of the hamper and saw six silver-grey chickens with fluffy plumage that looked more like long, silky fur than feathers.

'I'll find out,' he said, and went to ask Kerry.

'Ah, that'll be the Silkie hens,' she said. 'They're very special. They'll need to go in a separate enclosure from our chickens. Oh, look, more guests…'

A huge horsebox came swaying through the gate, missing the sides by only a couple of centimetres. Rory ran up to help the driver lower the big ramp.

 83

Inside the horsebox was the biggest horse Darren had ever seen. It was black, with fringes of white hair round its hooves, and a long white stripe down the front of its face.

'A Shire horse!' Jack was grinning from ear to ear. 'I've always wanted one of them.'

'This is Bessie,' Rory said. He told Jack to put her in the stable on the end of the row, which was the biggest one. Then he went back to the horsebox.

'Meet Thumbelina,' he said, as a tiny pony, not much bigger than a dog, trotted down the ramp. 'She's a Falabella – the smallest breed of horse in the world – and Bessie's best friend, apparently!'

Thumbelina gave a squeaky neigh, and went over to the stall next to Bessie's. She stood there, waiting for someone to let her in.

'There you go,' Darren said, unbolting the door and watching as the pony trotted in to explore her new home.

'Right,' Rory said, when they were all gathered together in the middle of the farmyard again. 'All our visitors are here. What we've got to do now is put the banner up. Darren, if you take one end of this...' Rory lifted up a roll of yellow fabric.

Darren helped him to unfurl the long, yellow

banner. It had big red letters on it, which said: *The Rare Breeds Show at City Farm. Everyone welcome!*

The two of them climbed up on ladders to fix the banner so that it hung high above the gate.

'That'll bring them in,' Rory said. Then he turned to Darren. 'Thanks for everything today. You've worked really hard. I don't think we'd have got it all done without you.'

Darren felt warm inside as he heard this. He looked around for Asha. He'd felt sick and miserable, earlier, when she wouldn't look at him or speak to him. But after he'd shown her his drawings she'd seemed much happier. And she'd been very friendly while they'd been cleaning out Charlie's enclosure. Maybe she'd forgiven him for last night.

Then he saw her. She was looking over the stable door at Thumbelina. 'It's hard to believe a pony could be so small,' she said, when Darren went up to her. 'Isn't she cute?'

'She's amazing,' Darren said. 'But look, she's too small to reach her food.'

The pony was so tiny she couldn't get her nose into the manger. Asha went to fetch a special little bucket for her to eat from.

When she came back, Darren said, 'What about

Basher?'

'Oh, no!' Asha clapped a hand to her mouth. 'Quick, let's go and clean him up.'

They hurried to the little goat's enclosure, where Rory had now added a couple of extra poles to the top of the fence.

Asha got a bucket of water, some shampoo, and a towel and they started cleaning the mud from Basher.

'Meh-eh-eh!' he said, as if he was really enjoying himself.

'I've had an idea,' Asha said. 'We should give Basher a collar. Then if he escapes again, it'll be easier to catch him. I could plait him one, from the string they tie hay bales with.' She looked up at Darren.

'Yeah, that's a great idea,' Darren said. Relief flooded through him, and he had to turn away and start rubbing Basher dry with the towel. Everything was OK. Asha didn't hate him, after all. She was still his friend. She had forgiven him, and everything was going to be all right.

Chapter Eight

'What are you up to this evening, Darren?' his dad asked. 'How about doing some of that homework the school set you?'

Darren and his parents were having their dinner at the kitchen table, before his mum went off to work.

The teachers at his school had given Darren some assignments to complete over the holidays, to catch up on work he had missed. So far, he hadn't even looked at them.

'OK, Dad,' Darren said. He was in such a good mood after his day at the farm that even the thought of tackling some maths didn't seem too bad.

When he'd finished eating, Darren went to his room and sat down at his desk. He got out the book his maths teacher had given him. *Algebra Made Easy*, it was called. It had explanations of how to do various problems, and then some examples that he was supposed to complete.

Easy? Darren thought, as he opened it up and read the first page. *They must be joking.*

He hated maths, especially algebra with all those stupid 'x's and 'y's. It was like some kind of language from outer space. He sighed, and shut the book again. Without someone to help him there was no chance he'd be able to finish any of the assignments.

It was very hot in the flat. The sun had been shining in for hours, and there was no breeze at all. Darren stared out of the window. The sky was very pale blue, almost white, from the heat, and there wasn't a cloud in sight.

He jumped up on the bed so that he could stick his head out of the top of the window, where it opened, and see what was going on down on the ground. Close to the entrance to the flats, someone was riding a bike round in small circles. Steven.

There was a tap on Darren's door. He leaped off the bed and sat down at the desk again.

'I'm off now, love.' His mum peered round the door. 'Be good, won't you?'

'Yup.'

Darren pretended he was studying *Algebra Made Easy*. His mum came in and kissed him on top of his head. 'Love you,' she said. 'Might see you at breakfast. If you're up.'

Breakfast was like an evening meal, for Mum, when she got home from her night shift at the hospital. But sometimes she was so tired that she just went straight to bed without eating anything at all.

'Ok,' Darren replied, turning a page. None of it made any sense to him at all. *If 'x' equals '2y'*... So what? Who cared? Darren hated maths so much he would rather be shovelling dirty straw back at the farm.

He heard his mum leave the flat, and then, far below, the sound of her feet walking over the car park towards the bus stop. He lay on his bed and read a couple of comic books, until the sky started to turn purple. The sun was setting at last. He got up and went to the bathroom.

Everything was very quiet in the flat. He looked round the living-room door, and saw his dad lying on the sofa with a newspaper over his face. Asleep again.

When he got back to his bedroom, he heard someone outside give a loud whistle. It could be Gary, trying to attract his attention. Darren got up on the bed and stuck his head out of the window again. Yes! There were his two mates, staring up at the flat.

Darren gave them a thumbs-up and headed out. His dad would be dead to the world for ages. He'd never notice he wasn't slaving away at maths homework.

'Hey, Daz!' Gary ran up and punched Darren on the shoulder. 'How's it going?'

'Cool,' Darren replied. It was great to be out of doors, and not stuck in his small, stuffy bedroom.

Steven skidded up to them and jumped off his BMX. 'Gazza's got a plan,' he said.

'What's that?'

Gary looked around the courtyard, and towards the parade of shops.

'We need to get out of here,' he said, nodding at the shops. 'They're watching us.'

Darren looked over at the shops. They were a sad-looking line-up. A late-night launderette with a metal grille over the front window, a greengrocer's where the fruit and veg always looked old and wrinkled, and the newsagents. Plus three other shops which had been closed down and had metal shutters over their front doors and windows.

'The geezer in the newsagents. He just came out. And the lady in the launderette – she's been spying on us the whole time.'

Darren could see a big woman, with her arms crossed, leaning against the door frame of the launderette. She was definitely looking their way.

'So…' Gary said with a grin. 'We need to go somewhere else. C'mon!'

Steven jumped on his bike to lead the way. They left the estate and went up the road by the park. Up ahead, Darren could see the tall gates of City Farm.

'Hang on,' Darren said. 'You don't mean… ?'

'Yeah, bro!' Gary said, his face glowing with excitement. 'It's the easiest place to break into. Just a stupid fence. And once we're in – we can do whatever we want.'

'No,' Darren said. 'No way.'

'Why not?' Steven said. 'There's no one in there at night. Only that old geezer with the white hair. He's the only one that lives there. And he'll never catch us.'

'That's right,' Gary said. 'C'mon, Daz!'

They were right outside the gates now. Darren couldn't see any way they could get in. The gates were very high and they were locked.

Steven veered to the right, and began pedalling along the wooden fence. Gary ran after him.

'Gazza!' Darren called. 'Leave it. OK?'

But he didn't listen. Darren followed them, his heart pounding. His friends still didn't know he'd been coming to the farm. So far he'd managed to fob them off with excuses, telling them he'd been helping his dad out with odd jobs during the daytime. A few hundred metres from the gate, one of the wooden fence panels was loose. Gary was tugging at it, helped by Steven.

'No – don't!' Darren said. His heart was beating painfully fast now. 'Please!'

Gary stopped pulling at the fence and turned to face him. '*Please?*' he mocked, copying Darren's voice. 'What's wrong with you, Daz? This is gonna be the best fun ever. C'mon, give us a hand.'

'No.'

Gary scowled at Darren. He turned back to the fence and attacked it ferociously. Half the panel broke off with a loud crack and fell to the ground. Darren could see inside the farm now. In the distance, he recognized the tree that stood by the pond. The place where'd he'd rescued Basher, earlier that day.

'Yeah!' Steven punched the air. 'Good one, Gazza!' He picked up his BMX and lifted it through the gap.

Gary followed him, grinning from ear to ear. Then he turned to Darren and beckoned him to come too.

Darren felt as if he was being torn in half. He'd never argued with his friends before. He'd always gone with them and joined in with whatever they were doing. But now his feet wouldn't move.

Gary's grin faded. 'What's up?'

'I can't,' Darren said. His voice felt so tight he could hardly speak.

Gary came back to the gap in the fence.

'Chicken!' he said.

'No, it's just…'

'Scaredy cat!' Steven squealed, pulling a stupid face.

Gary picked up a piece of the broken fence and chucked it at Darren. The splintery chunk of wood just missed him, falling to the ground at his feet.

'Wuss!' Gary yelled. Then he raced off towards the pond, with Steven pedalling after him.

Why hadn't they listened to him? Darren looked at the jagged hole in the fence. The night air was warm on his face, but he couldn't help shivering.

Please, please, he muttered to himself, clenching his fists, *don't let them do any harm…*

Even as he said this, he knew it was no good. Gary and Steven would do whatever they liked.

There was nothing he could do but go back home.

Chapter Nine

It was dark now, and really late, but Darren couldn't sleep. The lights in the car park below cast an eerie orange glow on the walls of his bedroom.

His thoughts tumbled around in his head. *What were Gary and Steven doing now? Were they still at the farm? What damage had they done?*

It probably wasn't anything *too* bad. Gary and Steven usually only did stupid things, like break bottles and the occasional window, and write on bins and walls. It would be OK. It *had* to be OK.

But Darren knew what his mates were like. Even if they didn't break anything, they were nosy. They'd be poking around the buildings and looking into the enclosures to see if there was anything they could steal.

And what if … Darren's heart leaped into this throat and he sat up in bed … *what if they found Basher's enclosure?*

The little goat would be able to look after himself, for sure. He'd just head-butt them, if they tried to catch him or hurt him. Darren smiled at the thought.

But supposing they left the gate open, and Basher escaped into the farm? What if he found the hole in the fence and got out of that too?

The little goat would probably head for the park – and on the other side of the park there was a busy dual carriageway. There was always traffic there, cars and massive lorries, even in the middle of the night. Basher would be killed instantly if he got hit by one of those lorries.

Darren couldn't lie still any longer. He had to go back to the farm and find out what was happening. He got up and pulled on his hoodie and his trackie bottoms. Next door, in his parents' bedroom, his dad gave a sudden shout.

'*Watch out! Stop!*'

Darren jumped. But then everything went quiet again, and he realized his dad was having one of his nightmares where he was back in the army again, and he and his mates were caught in an ambush.

Darren tiptoed out of his bedroom. He opened the door to his parents' room. The light was off, but he could just make out his dad tossing around in the bed and mumbling to himself.

'It's OK, Dad. It's just a dream,' Darren said. He'd heard his mum giving this reassurance so many times. 'It's all right. You're at home. Everyone's safe.'

'What?' Dad mumbled. 'Who's that?' He lifted his arm as if shielding his face.

Darren moved closer. His dad's eyes were tight shut. He was still fast asleep. Darren told him it was OK a few more times, and at last Dad fell quiet and lay back on the pillows.

For a moment Darren wished he could wake him up and tell him about Gary and Steven, and ask him to come to the farm. But his friends would never forgive him. They'd be in really big trouble if he turned up with his dad. He'd have to go it alone.

He slipped out of the flat and ran down the stairs. As he crossed the car park there was a loud clanging from the bins. Darren's heart jumped – maybe Gary and Steven had come back!

He looked round for them, but all he saw was a dog-like silhouette poised on the rim of one of the bins. It was an urban fox, rummaging for food in the rubbish.

Darren turned and headed for the farm, his trainers pounding the pavement.

When he got to the gap in the fence and peered through, everything was completely still. Not even a mouse moved in the bushes. He climbed in.

'Gazza?' he called in a low voice. 'Hey – Steven! You there?'

There was no reply. Darren ran towards the pond, moving silently as a shadow. There were some lamps along the path, giving off a weak yellow light, but his mates were nowhere to be seen. He stood under the tree and held his breath to listen, but there was nothing to hear.

He hurried on down the path towards the farmyard and Basher's pen. The gate was half-open, and his whole body turned cold as he saw that someone had been in and kicked over Basher's water bucket.

Then he heard a rustle from inside the little shed where he and Asha had piled up loads of clean straw to make a bed.

'Basher?' he whispered.

'Meh-eh-eh!' came the reply. The goat sounded very sleepy.

Darren went inside. It was quite dark, but he could

recognize Basher by his white patches. He fell down on his knees in the straw.

'Oh, mate,' he gasped. 'You're OK!'

Basher didn't bother to get up, but he head-butted Darren's arm as if to say: "Course I am! What d'you expect?'

Darren sat with the little goat for a while. Then he got his phone out of his pocket and looked at the time. It was past midnight. He should go home, in case his dad woke and decided to check up on him.

He'd just got back to the pond when a bright light flashed behind him, and a loud voice shouted: 'Who's there?'

Darren glanced over his shoulder and froze with fear. A tall man was running down the path after him.

It was Rory.

'Stop where you are!' he ordered Darren, shining the torch right into his face. 'What's going on?'

Darren blinked, shielding his eyes from the light. Rory sounded really angry, just like the headmaster when he caught Darren doing the graffiti on the bike shed. But this time, he wasn't doing anything wrong.

'Well?' Rory continued. 'Explain yourself, lad.'

'I came to—' Darren began, but his tongue kept tripping over itself. 'I came to check on Basher.'

'Why?' Rory frowned. He set off towards the farmyard and Basher's pen.

'He's fine, he's really OK,' Darren said, hurrying after him.

'But why were you so concerned?' Rory asked in a suspicious tone, opening Basher's gate and flashing the torch at the shed.

Darren was just trying to think of something to say in reply to this, when he heard Rory gasp.

'What the—?'

The torch beam flashed over the high farmyard wall behind the shed. The bricks were covered in graffiti. Nothing of the wall was still visible; it had all vanished beneath jagged lines and lurid colours.

Below the graffiti, a pile of tattered yellow fabric had been thrown over the roof of Basher's shed. It was the banner that Darren had helped Rory to put up that afternoon.

Darren groaned as he recognized Gary's tag on the wall – a little stick figure making a rude gesture. Steven's tag was there too – a BMX with two goggly eyes for wheels.

Rory walked over to turn on the big outside light from a switch on the barn wall. Now Darren could see the graffiti more clearly – a horrid mess of jumbled-up colours. Red and brown and yellow with big splodges of black.

'So this is why you were here,' Rory said in a grim voice, staring up at the wall.

To his horror, Darren saw that his friends had added *DAZ WOZ ERE* at the side of the graffiti.

'That's not my writing,' he gabbled. 'My tag's different, not like that at all …'

Rory wasn't listening. He just carried on looking at the graffiti. Then he turned to Darren. His face looked half angry and half sad.

Darren's legs felt weak. *I've got to explain. I've got to tell him what really happened*, he thought.

But his tongue felt like Charlie the bull was treading on it. It just couldn't move to form the words that he needed to say.

Chapter Ten

Rory's face was cold and hard as a stone as he stared at the ripped banner, and the wall daubed with messy colours.

'I know what you did at your school, Darren,' he said in a grave voice. 'They told me everything.'

'It wasn't me…' Darren struggled to defend himself.

Rory carried on speaking. 'When a new person comes to the Harvest Hope project, I don't think about their past. I like to take people as I find them.'

'I didn't do this…'

'I trusted you, lad. You've really let me down. We'll have to close the farm while we clean up the wall. We can't have young children see it like that.'

'I haven't let you down … I can explain.'

'Don't make it worse by lying to me.'

Rory switched off the torch and walked through the floodlit yard to the big gates. He started unbolting them. Then he told Darren to leave.

'Don't bother coming back,' he added, holding the gates open.

'Please…' Darren said. 'I only came to see Basher…'

'Too late for excuses, lad. Why would you break into the farm just to see that goat? There's nothing the matter with him.'

'My mates were—' Darren began to explain about Gary and Steven and then he stopped himself. He couldn't grass on his friends, even though he hated what they'd done.

Rory raised his white eyebrows as he waited for Darren to finish the sentence. Then he shook his head in exasperation.

'I'll explain to Kerry in the morning that you are no longer part of the project. Jack and Asha will be gutted,' he said.

Asha! Darren felt cold as he thought of her. She'd be really upset when they told her that he'd done that ugly graffiti and ruined the wall. She'd feel like he'd betrayed her…

'Come on, out!' Rory said. 'And don't show your face here again.'

Darren had no choice. He stumbled out through the gates and heard Rory clang them shut behind him. There was nothing to do but walk slowly back to the estate, climb the stairs in his block, and let himself into the flat.

He lay down on his bed. All was quiet. His dad's nightmare seemed to be over; he was snoring peacefully away on the other side of the wall. But there was no rest for Darren.

He couldn't help remembering Asha's face, when they'd been sitting at the table together that morning. She'd looked really unhappy, as if she was scared of him. As if he was a bad person. Now she'd believe that was true. She'd forget about how they'd worked together and had so much fun.

And what about the posters? He'd been looking forward to helping her with them. He could've come up with some really good designs. Lots of people would've seen them and then come to the Rare Breeds Show, and paid entrance fees. The farm would've made loads of money.

Darren groaned out loud as he thought of the show. He'd been really looking forward to doing his circus act with Basher. He'd even got his body warmer out from the wardrobe, all ready for the riding-on-

Darren's-back routine.

His mind ran round and round in circles, like a hamster he'd once had that used to spin its wheel, chasing crazily through the night.

At last the sky started to get light, and the birds began to chirp over in the park, warming up for their dawn chorus.

Then the front door clicked, and he heard his mum yawn as she arrived home from her night shift. He went through into the kitchen and filled the kettle.

'You're up early, Daz!' she said, dropping her bag on the floor and rubbing her eyes. 'Shall we have some cornflakes?'

Darren shook his head. He didn't like cereal much.

'Toast?'

'I'll make it,' Darren offered, as his mum sat down at the kitchen table and yawned again.

He stuffed four slices of bread in the toaster, and then he put a pan on the stove, opened a can of beans and plopped them into the pan. The way his mum was looking, she was about to fall into bed without eating again, like she did most mornings.

'Beans on toast! You're lovely, son,' she said, sniffing the warm smell that wafted up from the pan.

He poured hot water over a tea bag in her mug,

and gave it to her.

'I'm glad you like the farm,' she said. 'It's a wonderful place.'

It was warm in the kitchen, but Darren shivered. A cold pain gripped his chest as he realized that Rory would be getting up now to make the first inspection of the animals. And Asha and Jack would be eating their breakfast, and feeling excited about the day ahead – and the show too.

'What's up, love?' his mum asked, as he passed her the milk.

He almost told her about last night, but then he looked at her tired face. She would be really upset, and it wasn't fair to worry her when she was just about to go to sleep.

'Nothing,' he said.

He served up the beans on toast and hurried out of the kitchen, leaving his own plate uneaten on the table. He went to his room and sat on the bed. The sketchbook lay on the floor and he picked it up.

It fell open at his drawing of Basher wearing the shades, and the pain inside him got so bad he had to double over. He *had* to see the little goat again. Before he'd come to the farm he never would have thought he could care so much about an animal. But what could he do to put everything right? Suddenly, as if a light bulb had been switched on in his head, Darren had the answer.

Asha's dad was standing outside the newsagents, talking to a customer. He smiled when he saw Darren running past, and raised a hand in a friendly wave.

Darren flinched with embarrassment. Asha must have been telling him stuff. Saying what a nice boy he was. Talking about his artwork, and the fun they'd had training Basher.

Mr Gupta wouldn't be so friendly when he learned about last night. About the horrible graffiti. Darren's only hope of making everything all right again was to get his master plan to work.

Gary lived on the top floor of his block, so Darren took the lift up there. Luckily, the lift was working today, though it didn't smell that great. It was always a bit pongy until the cleaners came to do the weekly scrub-out.

Gary's big sister, Sarah, came to the door in her dressing gown. She told Darren that Gary was still in bed.

'I'll wait,' Darren said. 'It's important.'

Sarah looked at him as if he was mad, but she went

back inside the flat to deliver the message. Darren waited on the walkway until Gary came out in his tracksuit, rubbing his eyes.

'What's up, Daz?' he asked. 'I was asleep.'

'I need you to come with me.'

'What was last night about?' Gary asked. 'We thought you'd lost your bottle, big time.'

'No.'

'So why d'you run off like that? Not like you to turn chicken.'

'I wasn't being chicken. I can explain, Gazza. But – I need you to come with me.' Darren shifted from foot to foot while Gary made up his mind.

'What about Steve?'

'Yes, him too. Let's get him.'

Steven lived on the same floor as Gary. He was up already, eating his breakfast.

'Where're we going?' he asked, as they ran down the stairs. It was a long way down, but Darren didn't fancy the lift again.

Darren said he would tell them soon. All they had to do was trust him, and follow him.

As they ran past the block on their way out of the estate, Darren's dad was getting into his car to drive to work.

 107

'Darren!' he shouted. 'Come here!'

Darren's heart sank. But it was no use pretending he hadn't heard.

'Hold on a mo,' he said to the other two, and went over to the car.

'What've you been playing at?' his dad said, when Darren reached him.

Had Rory phoned his dad about the graffiti already? Dad looked annoyed, but not too angry, so hopefully he hadn't. Darren decided not to say anything.

'You said you'd do your homework,' Dad continued, 'but I checked your book of maths assignments this morning. You didn't finish a single one!'

Darren shut his eyes. He'd have stuck his fingers in his ears too, if he hadn't known that would make his dad completely furious.

'Sorry,' he said.

'Sorry's not good enough. You'll never get anywhere if you don't work at your lessons. How many times have I got to tell you?'

'I'm no good at maths…' Darren began. 'I don't understand it…'

Dad got into the car and slammed the door. He obviously wasn't interested in Darren's excuses.

'What was all that about?' Gary asked, as the car

revved and drove off out of the entrance to the estate.

'Nothing,' Darren told him. 'Come on, let's go.'

He led the way onto the road that ran past the park.

'What's the big idea, Daz?' Gary looked around warily as they walked up to the tall gates of City Farm.

'Trust me, it'll be OK,' Darren said, though he felt sick with nerves.

'We shouldn't be here!' Steven looked scared. 'If they see us, they might think it was us that—'

'Shut up!' Gary punched Steven's arm. 'Us that what, stupid? We didn't do anything, did we?'

'You did.' Darren looked Gary in the eye. 'I came back here, last night, and I saw your graffiti. And the torn-up banner too.'

'So what?' Gary scowled back at him.

Darren swallowed. 'This place is cool,' he said. 'I've been coming here, doing stuff with them, all week. That's why I didn't break in with you last night.'

'You're kidding!' Gary looked at Darren as if he'd just said he'd spent a week on Mars.

Darren assured him he was telling the truth. He explained how Rory had caught him, and accused him of doing the graffiti.

'They've kicked me out, Gazza. But the people here

are all right, I know they are. If we go to them now, and tell them what happened, and say we'll clean it all up…'

'Me?' Steven said, an expression of horror on his face. 'Clean up? Never.'

Gary gave a squeal of laughter and bent over double, clutching his belly. 'Daz, you're killing me!' he chortled. 'D'you really think… ?'

'Please, it'll be OK. If we just…'

Darren's mates were both laughing hysterically now. An icy shiver ran over Darren's skin. His plan wasn't going to work. They had no intention of helping him.

A small figure was walking across the farmyard, approaching the gates. Asha.

'Run!' Steven gasped.

And the two of them scarpered, racing up the road like their lives depended on it.

Gary and Steven had deserted him! Darren was so hurt he could hardly breathe. It was the same feeling he'd had once in a gym lesson, when he was vaulting over the horse and he'd miscalculated his jump, landing on top of it and winding himself. He leaned against the gate to steady himself.

'Are you all right?' Asha touched his elbow.

'Yup, I'm fine,' Darren managed to say, though he

didn't feel fine at all. He felt like the world was falling apart around him.

'Kerry's told me about last night. She said Rory had banned you from the farm,' Asha said. 'But I—'

'It wasn't me!' Darren's voice felt dry and hoarse.

'It was those two, wasn't it? The ones who just ran off. Your mates.'

She looked up at Darren, and he saw that she still trusted him. She was still his friend.

'I knew you couldn't have done it,' she continued. 'Come on. Let's go and explain.'

And Darren, feeling like he would rather have done anything than face Rory again, followed her in through the gates.

Chapter Eleven

'What's *he* doing here?' Jack said. 'He's banned!'

He sprang up from where he was sitting on the sofa, looking at Darren with an expression of disgust. Darren flinched. It was hard to believe that yesterday they'd been working together so happily.

Rory hurried over from the office area. 'I told you to stay away from here, Darren.'

'Hey!' Kerry came to join them. 'What's going on? Darren, you've been warned…'

'No, wait! It wasn't the way you think it was,' Asha's words came tumbling out too fast. 'It wasn't Darren's fault.' She gasped for breath.

Kerry told her to sit down. 'In fact, I think we all need to sit down,' she added, walking over to the sofa. 'Asha, take your time. We're all listening.'

Asha and Kerry sat on the sofa. Rory perched on one arm. Jack pulled up a chair next to him. Darren stayed on his feet. He didn't want to sit with them. Not until he knew that everything was going to be OK.

Asha took a deep breath. 'It was two other boys who did the graffiti,' she said. 'Darren's friends. They were here just now, but they ran away when they saw me.'

Rory frowned. 'Darren, how do you expect us to believe this? How come I caught you here last night?'

Darren's face was burning with shame. 'I didn't do it, honest,' he stammered. Then he explained how Gary and Steven had wanted him to join them, and how he'd refused. 'They called me chicken – but I wasn't scared. I just didn't want to do any harm…' Darren was so choked up that he couldn't speak for a moment.

'It's OK, Darren,' Kerry said.

Darren swallowed. 'I knew they'd got into the farm. I couldn't sleep; I was worried they might have hurt Basher, or let him escape. I didn't want him to run out on the road and get killed …'

'That's enough, lad,' Rory said. He got up from the arm of the sofa and gestured at Darren to come with him.

Darren followed him outside. His chest felt tight with sadness. Any moment now, Rory would throw him off the farm again and this time, Darren knew, he'd never be able to come back.

But Rory led Darren over to Basher's shed. He gazed up at the wall above, where the graffiti had been done. It looked even more vile in the sunshine.

Even though he hadn't actually done it, Darren still felt like the horrible mess on the wall was his fault. He should have tried harder to stop Gary and Steven and he knew that Rory must feel the same way.

The farm manager was rubbing his chin as he stared up at the graffiti. Then he turned to Darren. 'I've had an idea,' he said. 'We can't let our visitors see something like that. But the wall's a great spot for a mural. Could you fix it for us, lad?'

'What?' Darren gasped. He was still waiting for Rory to open the City Farm gates and chuck him out again.

'Well – could you clean it up, for starters? And then if I got you some paints and stuff, maybe you could design something. You know – a big picture of the farm. Something like that.'

'Of course! But...' For the second time this morning, Darren felt like he couldn't breathe. But this time, it was for a good reason. He was so happy it was making him all choked up.

'Right. Go and ask Kerry for a scrubbing brush and some cleaning stuff,' Rory told him. 'Oh, and Darren?'

'Yes.'

'I'm sorry I didn't listen to you last night. When I saw you here I jumped to conclusions and that was wrong.' Rory held out one of his big weather-beaten hands. Darren shook it nervously. He couldn't believe that a grown-up was actually apologizing to him.

'All right, lad, off you go then.'

Darren hurried back to the barn. Asha jumped to her feet as he went in.

'What happened?' she asked.

'It's OK,' Darren said. 'Rory believes me.' He explained about the mural. 'I've got to clean up the wall though.'

Asha offered to help him, right away.

'Me too!' Jack said. He looked much more friendly now. 'It'll be great to have a picture of the farm up there. Everyone who comes into the farmyard will be able to see it.'

Darren felt warm inside as he heard this. But he couldn't let the two of them help him.

'I should get rid of the graffiti,' he said. 'It's my fault that it happened. I should have tried harder to stop my mates. And I need to show Rory where my mates broke in, so we can fix the fence.'

Asha looked as if she was about to argue with him, but Kerry came up with a bucket and a large brush.

'Leave it, Asha. Darren wants to take the responsibility for this. You two can help Rory instead.' She gave Darren the bucket and the brush. 'Good luck,' Kerry added with a grin. 'It's a tough job. I'll come out and see how you're getting on, later.'

It was very hot up on the roof of the shed. Sweat was running down Darren's back and dripping from his forehead as he scrubbed away at the graffiti. Some of the colours washed off after a few goes with the brush, but others were much harder to get rid of.

Every now and then his hand slipped off the brush and his knuckles scraped against the wall, but he kept going. He had to get rid of the whole thing before he could start on the mural.

'Hey!' Kerry was climbing up the stepladder and onto the roof. She had a big bottle of drinking water for Darren. 'I brought this too,' she said, pulling a metal scraper out of her jeans pocket. 'I thought you might need it.'

Darren took a long swig of the water. 'Thanks,' he said, reaching for the scraper.

Kerry held onto it. 'You've been working so hard. I thought I'd help you for a while,' she said, chipping away at some of the paint. 'But don't tell Jack and Asha.'

'No, it's my responsibility, like you said.' Darren held out his hand for the scraper. 'I should do it.'

'OK.' Kerry handed the scraper over. 'I'm really impressed with you, Darren,' she said. 'You're a very hard worker. And you really care about doing the right thing.'

Darren shrugged. 'Sometimes,' he said. He still couldn't bear to think about last night. 'Mostly I'm rubbish.'

'Don't be like that.'

Darren started using the scraper. It was much better than the brush. Great big lumps of paint were flaking off the wall now.

'I was rubbish, last night. I should have stopped them,' he told Kerry.

'You were in a difficult position. It's very tough to go against what your friends are doing, let alone make them stop. You tried. And that's the important thing.'

'I wish my dad thought like that,' Darren muttered.

Kerry asked him what he meant, and Darren told her about the maths homework that he couldn't do.

'I tried and tried. But I just can't understand it. I *hate* maths. What's the point of it?'

Kerry laughed. 'Don't get me started!' she said. 'I spend my life doing sums, just to make sure we've got enough money to keep the farm open.'

Darren stared at her. She didn't look like the kind of person who would be good at maths.

'Yeah, OK,' he said. 'But that's just *sums*. One plus one equals two…'

'It's a bit more complicated than that!' Kerry raised an eyebrow at him.

'The thing I really hate is algebra – "x" and "y" are the stupidest things ever.'

'Talk to Rory,' Kerry suggested.

Darren was surprised. Rory seemed even less likely than Kerry to be interested in maths. Especially stupid old algebra.

Kerry went on, 'He has to do a lot of calculations. How much food each animal needs. How many vitamin supplements. I think he works it out with an equation, using the animal's bodyweight. I don't know exactly how. But I bet he'll tell you.'

'Really?' Darren had never thought of maths as being something you might need on a farm. As something useful.

'Sure. And he'll be happy to help out, if there's anything you don't understand.'

Kerry offered once more to do some scraping, but Darren told her he was fine. He really wanted to finish the clean-up operation on his own.

When she'd gone, he started thinking about his design for the mural. The animals that lived full-time on the farm – like Dusty and Cynthia and Curly – should take centre stage. But it would be great to put some of the special rare-breed vistors in too. Like Charlie the bull – and Basher, of course!

And what about the people – the new friends he'd made on the farm? In his mind, Darren saw a huge mural taking shape. He put the scraper down and let himself drift into the place he always went to when he was imagining a new piece of artwork.

But something suddenly pulled him back. Something Kerry had just said. She'd called Gary and Steven his friends. Darren felt a sharp pain in his chest as he thought of them. He bit his lip, pushing the pain away.

Steven and Gary weren't his friends. Not any more.

Not after they ran off and left him. They were just two boys he used to hang out with, when he had nothing better to do. Darren grabbed the brush and scrubbed away the last traces of their nasty graffiti.

Asha, he thought, was a *real* friend. He couldn't believe how she had spoken up for him.

It was so hot today that Asha was actually quite glad to sit in the barn at lunch time, and finish working on Basher's collar.

She was plaiting it with three strands, just like the *rakhi* bracelets she'd made for her big brother. One strand was the orange twine that came from the hay bales, one was a pink ribbon her mum had given her, and one was a length of the white string her dad sold in the newsagents.

'That's pretty, Asha,' Kerry said. 'What is it? Looks like a giant friendship bracelet.'

'It is, kind of. It's a collar, for Basher.' Asha finished plaiting and tied off the ends. 'There. I'll go and try it on him now.'

When she arrived at Basher's enclosure, she gasped with surprise. The graffiti had all gone! The wall was completely clean, and Rory was passing some cans of paint up to Darren.

Basher came trotting up to her and sniffed at her pocket.

'I know what you're after!' she said, and gave him a mint. Then she slipped the collar round the little goat's neck. The bright colours looked fantastic against his black and white coat. She'd plaited a lead for him too, with a loop at one end.

Now she slipped the lead through the collar, passing the other end through the loop so it was secure.

'Let's go and see what Darren's doing,' she said, and led the little goat outside into the bright sunshine.

'Hi!' Darren called down from the roof of the shed. 'Want to help with the mural?'

'No way!' Asha shook her head. 'I'm so bad at art.'

'Hey! What's that round Basher's neck?' Darren grinned down at the goat.

Asha explained that she'd made the collar for him. 'It's like a friendship bracelet,' she said, remembering Kerry's words.

'Cool!' Darren said. He picked up a paintbrush and dipped it in some black paint. 'OK. If I'm going to finish in time, I really need you to help out, Asha.'

'But I can't draw!'

'Remember – it's all about shapes. Watch.'

He outlined a big oval shape on the wall.

'Who's this?'

'I don't know!' Asha stared as Darren added a triangle to one end of the oval. And then a little spiral at the other end.

'Oh – I know! It's Cynthia! That's her head – and that curly thing is her tail.'

Darren added four legs to the pig's body, and a mouth, eyes and ears to her head. Then he moved along the wall and began another outline – a big rectangle.

'How about this one?' he called down.

Asha frowned. She didn't recognize the shape at all. It certainly wasn't one of the regular animals at City Farm.

Darren added a wide triangle at one end, with two little eyes. He looked over his shoulder at Asha. 'Still don't know?'

'Got it!' Asha shouted. 'It's Charlie the bull.'

Darren sketched in a few more animals. Curly the sheep, Stanley the pony and Dusty the donkey all came to life on the wall as he drew their outlines in the thick black paint.

Then he started on something different. Asha stared. There was a circle. And an oval, underneath the circle. What kind of animal was that?

Darren added two long thin sausage-shapes coming out of the oval at the sides and two similar shapes at the bottom.

Asha caught her breath. Now she understood. 'It's a person!' she called up to him.

'Yeah – but who?'

'Give me a clue.'

'It's someone important.'

Asha watched as Darren added a small circle, with five little sausages attached, onto the end of both the arms.

'Come on, guess!' he said.

'Rory? Kerry?' Asha asked. But she had no idea who it was. The figure Darren was sketching could be anyone.

Now Darren was adding feet to the ends of the legs.

'Someone *really* important,' he said, as he moved the brush back to the figure's head.

'Oh!' Asha gasped. Darren was drawing a headscarf. 'It's me!'

'Yup!' Darren grinned at her.

Asha burst out laughing. It was amazing to see herself up there on the wall. And the drawing *was* just like her. Darren was adding details to the face, and the expression was perfect – just as if the drawing was about to start giggling.

'You're a genius!'

'Maybe,' Darren said with a grin. 'But I'll never get this done unless you help me. Come on up and fill these outlines in with some colour.'

Smiling, Asha put Basher back in his shed and climbed up the ladder onto the roof.

'And when you've done that,' Darren said, 'I'm going to show you how to draw a chicken, OK? Cos we'll need loads of them, running around everywhere.'

Asha picked up a brush, dipped it in some brown paint and got to work adding some colour to Charlie the bull.

She didn't feel so shy about drawing now. In fact, she felt excited. Darren was so brilliant – he'd show her exactly how to do it. The chickens would look great, really lifelike. This time, everyone would know exactly what it was she had drawn and, for once, no one would laugh at it.

Chapter Twelve

A week later, it was the hottest day of the summer so far. The Rare Breeds Show had been open for about two hours, and the farmyard buzzed with excited chatter as children flocked to see 'the Amazing Superstar Balthazar'.

'OK, everyone. The next performance is about to begin,' Darren said, eyeing the queue outside Basher's enclosure. 'I'll need five assistants. The rest can watch from the other side of the fence.'

Two boys and three girls put their hands up. Darren let them into the pen and showed them where to stand, each one by a different obstacle around the course he'd set up for Basher.

The obstacle course looked very intriguing, with a tall pyramid of hay bales, a brightly painted table and a hoop all plaited round with colourful ribbons.

'Is it a circus?' a little girl asked, standing on tiptoe to peer over the fence.

'Sort of.' Darren grinned as he handed out some treats to his five assistants.

He told the two boys to stand by the pyramid. One of the girls went by the table, one by the hoop, and the last girl was to stay by Darren's side.

'OK. When The Amazing Balthazar gets to your obstacle, you say "Up!",' Darren instructed them. 'After he's performed the trick, you give him a treat.'

'What about me?' the last girl asked. 'What's my trick?'

'Wait and see,' Darren said. 'It's the grand finale.'

He slipped his body warmer on over his T-shirt. Then he whistled to Basher.

Basher trotted out of the shed. He looked so cute, with his black and white patches freshly washed and the new collar round his neck, that a couple of the kids clapped, even though the performance hadn't begun yet.

Basher had practised his routine so many times that he knew exactly what was going to happen. He trotted over to the base of the pyramid.

One of the boys called out, 'Up!' and Basher

jumped onto the first bale. He got his treat, and then the other boy said, 'Up!' – and with one bound, the little goat was at the top of the pyramid.

The kids all cheered and yelled. Darren's heart swelled with pride as Basher sprang down from the pyramid and trotted over to the hoop.

As soon as the little goat heard the command, he leaped right through the hoop. This time he didn't even wait for his treat, but raced to the table and jumped up to pose on top of it. The audience applauded loudly.

'Isn't he clever?' the girl by the table said, as she gave Basher a double treat.

'And now, ladies and gentlemen, the grand finale!' Darren said.

He whispered a quick instruction to the girl who stood beside him, and then he knelt down on all fours.

Basher jumped off the table. Darren heard the straw rustle as he trotted over.

The girl cried, 'Up!' and then Darren felt the goat's little hooves on his back.

A cry of 'Ooooh!' went up from the audience, and then lots of cheers and whistles and another outburst of clapping as Darren crawled around the pen with Basher on top of him.

'Good boy,' Darren said, coming to a halt.

Basher jumped down and came round to stand in front of Darren. He dropped his head as if he was going to head-butt him.

'Easy,' Darren whispered, and pressed his forehead against Basher's.

'Aaaah!' the audience cried. 'That's so cute…'

Darren jumped to his feet and held out his arms. Basher jumped right into them. 'Ladies and Gentlemen – the Amazing Superstar Balthazar!' Darren said.

Then he put Basher back in the shed and thanked his five assistants, who all went out of the enclosure looking very happy.

'When's the next performance?' a boy in the audience called. 'Can I be in it?'

'Me too!' the little girl who'd been watching over the fence yelled. 'I want a go!'

'Can I hold him?' someone else shouted. 'Please, please!'

'Steady on!' Rory came striding across the farmyard. 'The Grand Parade is just about to start. Make your way up to the horses' field, or you'll miss the fun.'

The kids trooped out of the farmyard and Rory leaned over the fence. 'How's it going?'

Darren told him how brilliant Basher had been. 'He doesn't seem a bit tired. He's all ready to do another show!' he added, as Basher's black and white face peeped round the door of the shed to see what was going on.

Rory grinned. 'That's great. Because I'd like you and Basher to lead the parade.'

'No!' Darren exclaimed. 'It should be Asha. Or Jack. Not me.'

'I've spoken to the others, and we all agree that it should be you, lad. You've worked harder than anyone to make the show a success.'

'But I...' Darren suddenly felt very nervous. It was all right just him and Basher playing with the kids – but having to lead the parade, in front of all the visitors ... that was something else.

'See you up at the field in ten minutes!' Rory set off down the path.

Darren went into the shed. He sat down on the straw and rubbed Basher's forehead. 'You ready for this?' he asked.

The little goat head-butted him in the arm, and then tried to jump into his lap.

Darren burst out laughing. ''Course you are! You're Basher the Smasher, aren't you? You superstar!'

He looped the little goat's lead through his collar, and was just leading him out of the shed when he froze in his tracks. Someone was leaning on the gate. A man with a black beard and bushy eyebrows.

Darren couldn't believe his eyes. It was Mr Dodge, the teacher who'd called his artwork 'silly scribbling'. He was staring right at Darren.

Darren wished he could turn around and hide in Basher's shed. But then he and Basher would miss the parade. He'd have to face this one out. He clutched Basher's lead and took a step forward.

'Darren, isn't it?' Mr Dodge said in his deep voice. 'Thought I recognized you.'

He stared at the mural, high on the wall above the shed. At the colourful animals, the lively caricatures of Rory, Kerry, Asha and Jack, and the mother-hen shape of the old barn in the background, with its wings stretching out to embrace the whole farm.

The art teacher frowned and made an odd noise, halfway between a whistle and a sigh.

Darren cringed as he waited for Mr Dodge to say something rude about the mural. About how it wasn't 'realistic'. About how it was just a load of scribble.

'Who did that?' the teacher said after a long pause. 'I did.'

Darren could hardly speak. He felt like knocking Basher's pyramid down and burying himself under the hay.

'It's excellent,' Mr Dodge said.

'What?'

'Really good work. The way you've captured the attitude of each animal – and the characters of the humans. They just leap out from the wall as you look at them.'

'Oh, um…' Darren stammered. His brain could hardly take in what he'd just heard, let alone think of a suitable reply.

'You designed those posters too, didn't you? The ones that advertise the show? They're fantastic. You should get some reproductions made,' Mr Dodge continued. 'Cards that people could buy. Souvenirs. That'd be a great money-maker for this place.'

'Right!' Darren gasped.

Mr Dodge raised an eyebrow at him, and wandered off across the farmyard to look at the chickens.

Darren was so happy he felt as if he might burst. The art teacher liked his mural! And his posters! '*Fantastic!*' he'd said.

Suddenly the idea of leading the Grand Parade didn't seem daunting at all. Darren opened the gate, and hurried to the horses' field, with Basher trotting at his heels.

*

'That was the best day ever,' Asha sighed, as she pinned up a large rosette over the door of Basher's shed.

Printed on the rosette were the words: *City Farm Rare Breeds Show – Cleverest Animal*.

'He'd have won "Cutest Animal" too, if it hadn't been for the alpacas,' she added.

Asha had led the mother and baby alpaca in the Grand Parade, and she'd been thrilled when they won a rosette. But she didn't want Basher to feel left out. He was ever so cute too.

Darren laughed. 'He'd rather win the prize for cleverest, any day. Wouldn't you, mate?'

Basher was too busy chewing his way through a mega-bowl of chopped carrots and apples to reply.

'He's the top "kid" on the block!' Asha giggled.

'That's right,' Darren replied. 'And he's definitely got the coolest collar.'

Asha felt her face go warm when he said this. She was really pleased that Darren liked her 'friendship' collar.

'We all thought Rory would lead Charlie the bull,' she continued, changing the subject, 'but Jack was brilliant, wasn't he? You could tell he used to live on a farm.'

'Yup.' Darren nodded.

Charlie the bull might have won the rosette for 'Strongest Animal', but he'd followed Jack round the field as quietly as a baby calf.

'Did your mum and dad like the show?' Asha asked.

Darren's mum and dad had been standing in the front row of the spectators, right up next to the fence, when the parade took place.

Darren nodded. He was full of emotion as he remembered what his dad had said to him after the parade.

'I'm proud of you, son. Really proud.' He'd never heard those words from his dad before. Dad's face had been very red as he added, 'To see you out in front there, Darren, leading everyone along, it was really something. Well done.' Then his dad had bent down to pat Basher. 'Hello, little 'un!' he'd said. 'Did you know, when I was in the army, our regimental mascot was a goat? Just like this little chap, only brown and white. I'm so proud of you, Darren.'

Mum had given Darren a hug, and then she'd hugged Basher, and then she'd hugged Darren again. She hadn't said much, because her eyes were welling up and she had to keep blowing her nose.

'Was your mum all right?' Asha asked now. 'I

thought I saw her crying.'

'She always does that,' Darren explained. 'She cried buckets when I was in the Nativity play at my junior school. It was really embarrassing.'

Asha smiled. 'My mum's just as bad! She never cried once when I was ill, but any time something good happens she's in floods!'

Darren grinned. 'Mum soon cheered up when Rory came over with Thumbelina! She was in hysterics. He's so tall, and she's so small – they looked really funny together.'

'Hilarious!' Asha started laughing so much she had to sit down on one of the hay bales. 'Thumbelina hardly comes up to Rory's knees! She and Bessie the Shire Horse definitely deserved the prize for "Best Little and Large".'

'Isn't it weird that Thumbelina is so friendly with such a large animal?' Darren said.

Asha smiled as she remembered how shocked Kerry had looked when she was leading Bessie in the parade and the massive horse had suddenly stopped in her tracks, almost knocking Kerry over. The huge horse had lost sight of her friend, Thumbelina. She'd let out a huge neigh, looking all around for the tiny pony. Luckily, the big horse calmed down as soon as they were allowed to walk side by side again.

It was so cute, the way that animals formed friendships, just like people. Good friendships, like she had with Jack – and now with Darren too. But friendships could go wrong, sometimes. Friends could behave badly. They could let you down.

Asha looked at Darren. He'd been a real star today, and all the kids who'd come to the show had thought he was brilliant. But he was only at the farm for one more week. What would he do when he had to leave and go back to school with those two boys from the estate?

'You know those friends of yours…' she began.

Darren frowned. 'What – Gary and Steven?'

'Yeah. Do you think you'll—'

'They're not my friends,' Darren said quickly. 'Not any more.'

'Really?' Asha felt a wave of happiness rise up inside her.

'Nope. Don't need them,' Darren continued. 'I've got two new friends, haven't I? Asha and Basher!'

Asha burst into giggles. And Basher, hearing the sound of his name, looked up from his bowl of treats and joined in with a loud, 'Meh-eh-eh!'

Epilogue

It was a Saturday in the autumn, and the leaves on the trees in the park were turning yellow and red and orange. Darren hurried along the road towards the City Farm gates.

'I hope you like the farm, miss,' he said, turning to Miss Hastings, who was walking beside him.

'I know I will,' she replied. 'I've heard so much about it – and your idea of bringing the kids from my art classes to draw the animals is brilliant.'

Darren had suggested this to his art teacher when she came back to school after the summer holidays. Now she was coming with him to discuss the plan with Rory and Kerry.

'I can't wait to see your mural,' she added. 'Mr Dodge was really impressed with it.'

Darren told her how he'd expected Mr Dodge to hate the mural. 'He really told me off in the art class. Said I was doing silly scribbling.'

Miss Hastings laughed. 'He's hard to please, isn't he? But when he praises you, he means it. Did you know that he was my art teacher when I was at college?'

Darren shook his head.

'That's why I suggested him to replace me when I was ill. We'll have a class outing, sometime soon, to the City Gallery, and you can see some of his paintings. I think you'll like them.'

Now they were at the gate and walking through into the farmyard. There was a rustle of straw and a loud 'Meh-eh-eh!' from Basher's pen. The goat stood on his hind legs and peered through the fence at them.

Darren pointed out the mural to Miss Hastings, and then he told her she'd find Kerry and Rory in the barn.

'I've got something to do,' he said, looking at Basher, who was trying to climb up the fence.

'So I see!' Miss Hastings smiled at the goat. 'A very important appointment, I can tell. The mural's stunning, Darren. I'll have another look later.'

She set off for the barn, and Darren opened the gate and went in to see Basher.

During the summer holidays he'd come to the farm every day, but he'd been so busy at school since the start of term that he hadn't had much chance to come and visit. Would the little goat remember him, now that he hadn't been for so long?

Basher was lying in the straw in his pen, but he jumped straight up when he saw Darren.

'Up!' Darren said, and Basher jumped straight into his arms, just like he used to do for the finale of their routine. 'Wow!' Darren staggered a couple of steps. Basher was quite a lot bigger than the last time he'd seen him. 'You're not so little now, mate!'

'Meh-eh!' Basher replied, and head-butted Darren's shoulder.

Darren put Basher down in the straw, and knelt so that they could lean up close together, forehead to forehead, like they used to do.

Darren gazed into Basher's yellow eyes. 'Looks like you haven't forgotten me,' he said.

Basher dropped his head to sniff Darren's hand.

'OK – I've brought you a mint!' Darren unwrapped the sweet and gave it to him.

'Hi, there!' Asha called, opening the gate and coming in to the enclosure. 'I'm so glad you're here. We've run out of postcards, completely!'

'No way!' Darren felt a rush of pride. Over the summer holidays, he'd created a range of postcards for the farm, based on the animal designs from his posters.

'Yes! Every single one's been sold.'

'Great!' Darren felt incredibly proud as he thought of all the people who now owned a card with one of his designs on it.

'Rory says we could have sold them all twice over,' Asha added.

Darren frowned as he started calculating a sum in his head. He'd been working really hard at maths since he and Rory had sat down and gone through his homework assignments together.

'The printers will do us a very good price for the next lot of cards if we order double the amount,' he told Asha after a moment. 'So that'll mean more profit for the farm.'

'Awesome!' Asha said. 'Kerry'll love that. Did you bring your sketchbook?'

'Of course!' Darren pulled the black book out of his bag.

''Cos I think we might need some new designs!'

Darren laughed. 'OK. What?'

'Well – I just walked past Cynthia's sty, and Jack

was playing football with her. It's amazing – he's taught her to save a goal! She does it every time. Can you believe it?'

'Anything is possible at City Farm.' Darren grinned. 'Remember the Amazing Superstar Balthazar? Basher the Smasher?' He scratched Basher's head, between his little horns.

'How could I forget?' Asha laughed. 'I bet you wouldn't let him jump on your back now though.'

'Well – maybe just this once.'

Darren got up down on all fours and Basher leaped straight onto his back.

'Steady, boy!' Darren said, gritting his teeth as he felt the goat's hooves through his coat. 'Stay still up there and I can just about manage to carry you!'

Asha clapped loudly. 'Yay! We should have that Superstar Balthazar trick on the new cards!'

'You'll have to draw it,' Darren said, ''cos I can't draw and pose at the same time. And you'll have to be quick – he's really heavy now.'

Basher leaped down again, and ran to Asha for a minty reward.

'Only if you show me how, and what shapes I need to use,' Asha said.

'No problem. But we'll do Cynthia and Jack first.

Come on, Asha, let's go and start the new range of City Farm postcards!'

CHARACTER PROFILE

ANIMAL: Pygmy goat
ANIMAL NAME: Basher

LIKES:
Doing tricks and getting lots of attention.

DISLIKES:
Being stuck in his pen.

FAVOURITE PLACE:
Wherever he's not supposed to be!

FAVOURITE FOOD:
Carrots and apples, but he'll try to eat anything.

Read on for a sneak peek of the next City
Farm adventure…

Katie *and the* **Ducklings**

Katie dragged her school sweatshirt from the dirty washing basket and tried to ignore its stale smell. Mum hadn't got round to doing any washing all weekend but Katie didn't want to complain because she didn't want to upset her. It was hard enough getting Mum out of bed to drive her to school these days; if she complained about her smelly sweatshirt, Mum might just hide under the covers again.

Katie picked the crusty ketchup off the sleeve and brushed out the chalk marks, then she peeked out of her bedroom, wishing she could smell breakfast cooking. But there was only the smell of last night's fish fingers. The hall light wasn't even on. Mum must still be in bed. Padding softly to the bathroom, Katie reached for her toothbrush, squeezed out some toothpaste and began cleaning her teeth. A few months ago, Mum would have been downstairs by now, singing along to the radio while she whipped up a batch of muffins or a stack of pancakes. Mum loved cooking, and she always used to pile the breakfast table with delicious treats to make Katie smile before school.

That's how it used to be. Now Katie felt like her old mum was disappearing. It was scary. Katie had no dad to fill in the gaps. If Mum disappeared, she'd be all alone.

She pushed the thought away and spat out the toothpaste.

If only Mum hadn't lost her job.

That's when everything had started to change. Mum hadn't stopped baking straightaway. Katie stared wistfully into the bathroom mirror as she remembered Mum's double-chocolate-chip-marble-cheesecake and her super-special-cupcakes whirled with icing and sparkling with sprinkles. When she'd first lost her job, Mum had seemed more filled with energy than ever, applying for jobs and travelling to interviews. There was always a pile of job application forms stacked neatly on the dining-room table, usually next to a plate full of freshly baked buns. But gradually Mum had stopped looking for work. Then she'd stopped baking. Now she hardly left the house. She hardly left her bed.

Please let Mum get up today and take me to school. Katie brushed her teeth harder. *If I scrub off every bit of plaque*, Katie begged the Tooth Fairy, *please make her get up and drive me to school.* Of course Katie knew the Tooth Fairy didn't exist. She was nearly eleven. But there was no one else to ask. She rinsed her mouth out with water. She couldn't miss this week's spelling test. She'd missed last week's test; Mum hadn't felt well enough to get up and drive her to school. This week Katie had learned every word on her spelling list. She was determined to prove that she could keep up, even though she'd missed so many lessons recently.

If only school was closer, she could walk there. Katie put her toothbrush back into the pot beside the tap. Perhaps she could learn to take the bus. But Mum had stopped giving her pocket money weeks ago so she didn't have any money for her bus fare.

She came out of the bathroom and looked at her watch. Eight o'clock. Mum's room was still dark. Then Katie had an idea. Creeping downstairs, she flicked on the kitchen light. The weather outside looked chilly and dull. Katie tucked her feet into her fluffy slippers and put the kettle on. If she woke Mum with a nice cup of coffee, it might cheer her up; and then she'd get up and drive Katie to school in time for registration.

Nervously, Katie waited while the kettle rumbled to a boil. She reached into the cupboard for the coffee jar and spooned some into a mug. Tipping the kettle carefully, she filled the mug, added a splash of milk from the fridge and carried the coffee carefully upstairs.

'Mum?' She paused outside Mum's bedroom door, and then pushed it open. Inside was dark and it smelled fusty, like Katie's sweatshirt.

On the ruffled bed, a mound of duvet moved a little.

'Mum?' Katie tiptoed closer. 'I've brought you a cup of coffee.'

Mum peered over the duvet and rubbed her eyes. 'What?'

'I hope it's going to be sunny later,' Katie said brightly, ignoring the dark rings under Mum's eyes. 'Because it's games this afternoon and we're playing football on the outdoor pitch.' She carefully stepped over a pile of clothes heaped beside the bed. Clearing a space on the cluttered bedside table, she put down the coffee. The mug was starting to burn her fingers.

'Hello, love.' Katie recognized Mum's pretend-happy voice. Mum heaved herself up into a sitting position and piled some pillows behind her head before sinking back against them.

'Shall I open a window?' Katie asked. Maybe some fresh air might make her mum want to go outside.

'What time is it?' Mum yawned.

Hope flickered in Katie's chest as she made a crack between the curtains and opened the window just wide enough to let in a little air. 'Quarter past eight. If you get up now we can still get to school on time.'

Mum sighed. 'School.' She looked wearily at Katie. 'I'm not really feeling too good, Katie. Why don't you stay home today? You can always do some reading here.'

'I have to go.' Katie stared at her mum. 'I have a spelling test.'

Mum frowned. 'But I'm not feeling well enough to drive.'

'You look OK.' Katie picked up the mug of coffee. If she could just get her mum to take a sip she might feel a bit better. Katie knew her mum wasn't actually ill. Her sadness had just got so big it felt too heavy to move. 'Here.' She held out the coffee.

But Mum didn't see it. She was too busy rubbing

her eyes. Katie gasped as Mum's elbow collided with the mug, sending coffee splashing across the duvet.

Katie froze. She watched the brown liquid spread over the cream cotton and sink in. 'I'm sorry!' she cried.

Mum's face crumpled. 'Oh no! Look at the mess. What am I going to do?'

Katie felt her throat tighten. Why couldn't Mum go back to being the nice mum who made pancakes and buns and who always knew what to do? 'I'm really sorry.' She felt her lip start to tremble. 'I was just trying to—'

'Please! Leave me alone. I told you, I'm not feeling well. I just need to be left in peace.' Mum wriggled back under the coffee-stained duvet.

'But what about school?'

'It won't hurt you to miss it for once,' Mum mumbled from beneath the duvet.

'But it's not just once! It's nearly every day!' Angrily, Katie fumbled for the door behind her. Tears spilled down her cheeks as she raced for her bedroom, choking back sobs.

Read

Katie and the **Ducklings**

to find out what happens next!

HANDBOOK

City Farm Rules:

Lots of people visit City Farm everyday. Follow these simple rules to make sure that everyone enjoys themselves.

- Treat people – and animals – with respect and kindness.

- Help out and join in! If you can see someone needs a hand, offer to help them.

- Don't feed the animals, some of them are on special diets, and different food will upset their tummies.

- Wash your hands! Most of the City Farm animals like to be held and stroked, but you should always wash your hands afterwards.

- Have fun!

1

Our Guinea Pigs:

Bubble and Squeak are our guinea pigs. They're very friendly and love being held and petted every day.

🐾 Guinea pigs originally come from South America and usually live until they are five or six years old.

🐾 Guinea pigs are very social creatures and Bubble and Squeak would get very lonely if they didn't have each other. They like having lots of hay and straw to burrow in, and toilet-roll tubes to use as tunnels.

🐾 Guinea pigs are active up to 20 hours per day and sleep only for short periods.

🐾 Guinea pigs make lots of different noises which mean different things. When they're excited they make lots of squeaking 'wheek' sounds and they purr when they're being stroked.

Our Equines:

*City Farm is lucky enough to have a pony called Stanley,
an ex-racehorse called Swift and a donkey called Dusty. Horses
and donkeys take a lot of looking after.*

U Our horses and donkeys need to be mucked out every morning, and given a pile of fresh straw for their beds.

U They have small feeds at breakfast and lunchtime, and each have a net full of hay in the evening. During the day they are 'turned out' into the field for at least six hours so that they can graze on the grass.

U We always check that there are no holes in the fencing, and no broken glass or poisonous plants before they are turned out into the paddock.

U In the winter, Dusty, Stanley and Swift have stable rugs on their backs so they don't get cold.

Our Pig:

Cynthia is City Farm's Tamworth pig. She loves playing football!

👣 Pigs are actually very clean. When Cynthia rolls in the mud it's because she's hot. Pigs can't sweat, so they cover themselves in cool mud, which cools them down and protects their skin from the sun.

👣 Pigs are also very smart, and they learn tricks faster than dogs. They like to have toys like a football to keep them entertained.

👣 Tamworth pigs are a gingery-orange colour, and they originally come from the UK.

👣 Pigs have such a good sense of smell that they can find things buried underground.

👣 It is actually illegal to give pigs scraps from the kitchen.

Our Goats:

City Farm has five goats – dairy goats Nelly and Nancy, male goats Billy and Bramble, and a new goat, naughty little Basher.

◖ Dairy goats need milking every day. More people in the world drink goats' milk than cows' milk. Goat's milk makes delicious cheeses.

◖ Goats can live between 12 and 16 years.

◖ Goats only have teeth on their bottom jaw, the top is a hard palate.

◖ Goats are often very good at escaping their pens – like Basher – so we have to make sure their enclosures are secure.

◖ Baby goats are called kids, and goats can have up to six kids per litter.

OUR CHICKENS AND DUCKS:

There are lots of chickens and ducks at City Farm, and more ducklings and chicks hatch every year.

Chickens and ducks need a shed to sleep in at night, otherwise they might get eaten by foxes.

Very few ducks actually "quack", but ducks do make a wide range of noises.

Ducks have webbed feet that act like paddles, and their feathers are waterproof.

Chickens preen their feathers every day, and like to take dust baths in the farmyard.

Our *City Farm* and the *Harvest Hope* project
are fictional, but there are real city farms
all around the country and they often
need volunteers. Why not go and visit the
one nearest to you?